Samuel French Acting Edition

I0591803

The Doctor in Wonderland

by Don Zolidis

SAMUELFRENCH.COM   SAMUELFRENCH.CO.UK

FOR PRODUCTION ENQUIRIES

UNITED STATES AND CANADA
Info@SamuelFrench.com
1-866-598-8449

UNITED KINGDOM AND EUROPE
Plays@SamuelFrench.co.uk
020-7255-4302

Each title is subject to availability from Samuel French, depending upon country of performance. Please be aware that *THE DOCTOR IN WONDERLAND* may not be licensed by Samuel French in your territory. Professional and amateur producers should contact the nearest Samuel French office or licensing partner to verify availability.

MUSIC USE NOTE

Licensees are solely responsible for obtaining formal written permission from copyright owners to use copyrighted music in the performance of this play and are strongly cautioned to do so. If no such permission is obtained by the licensee, then the licensee must use only original music that the licensee owns and controls. Licensees are solely responsible and liable for all music clearances and shall indemnify the copyright owners of the play(s) and their licensing agent, Samuel French, against any costs, expenses, losses and liabilities arising from the use of music by licensees. Please contact the appropriate music licensing authority in your territory for the rights to any incidental music.

IMPORTANT BILLING AND CREDIT REQUIREMENTS

If you have obtained performance rights to this title, please refer to your licensing agreement for important billing and credit requirements.

THE DOCTOR IN WONDERLAND was first presented at Cedar Valley Middle School in Round Rock, Texas on November 3, 2016. It was directed by Kris Baker. The original cast was as follows:

DOCTOR WHAT....................................Daniel Konatham
CARA .... Maddie Baker
WHITE RABBIT / ROBOT 2................................ Kyla Lee
MAD HATTER ....Jackson McCalmont
DORMOUSE / KNAVE OF HEARTS........................ Rhea Jain
MARCH HARE .... Sharada Rao
CATERPILLAR / MOTHER............................ Delaney Estes
MOCK TURTLE / GRYPHON.........................Claire Fleming
PANSY / FIVE OF HEARTS......................... Himanshi Malik
DANDELION / NINE OF HEARTS .... Becky Haag
POPPY / SEVEN OF HEARTS ....Julie Patel
WALRUS... Catherine Stephen
DODO / JABBERWOCK .... Hal Fukushima
CHESHIRE CAT ....Kami Dishinger
HUMPTY DUMPTY / ROBOT 3.......................Quentin Arvizu
FOUR OF HEARTS / RED KING .... Xander Hinze
TWEEDLEDEE............................... Udhaya Selvamurugan
TWEEDLEDUM.................................... Noor Elkenaney
RED QUEEN / ROBOT 1 .... Evelyn Tjoa

ADDITIONAL PRODUCTION HISTORY

Cedar Valley Middle School, Round Rock, Texas: October, 2016
Kids-N-Co, El Paso, Texas: October 30-November 9, 2016
Adna High School, Adna, Washington: November 16, 2016
Cocke County High School, Newport, Tennessee: November 18-20, 2016
Glenville State College, Glenville, West Virginia: December 1-3, 2016
Fannin Middle School, Amarillo, Texas: December 1-31, 2016

CHARACTERS

DOCTOR WHAT – (Referred to as **"THE DOCTOR."**) An interdimensional traveler. A bit acerbic and sarcastic.

CARA – His assistant, a wide-eyed girl from present day England.

WHITE RABBIT – (male or female) A giant rabbit. The Queen's Trumpeter.

MAD HATTER – (male) An insane haberdasher.

DORMOUSE – (male or female) A narcoleptic rodent.

MARCH HARE – (male or female) A devious rabbit.

CATERPILLAR – (male or female) A grub marriage counselor.

MOCK TURTLE – Not a real turtle, pretty sad about it.

PANSY – (male or female) A mechanical flower.

DANDELION – (male or female) A mechanical flower.

POPPY – (male or female) A mechanical flower.

WALRUS – (female) A genius inventor. Also a walrus.

DODO – (male or female) An extinct bird, the Walrus' assistant.

CHESHIRE CAT – (female) A disappearing feline.

HUMPTY DUMPTY – (male or female) The high executioner. Also an egg.

TWEEDLEDEE – A thug.

TWEEDLEDUM – Another thug.

JABBERWOCK

RED QUEEN – Queen of Wonderland. A demagogue.

RED KING – Asleep, dreaming.

KNAVE OF HEARTS

FOUR OF HEARTS

SEVEN OF HEARTS

FIVE OF HEARTS

NINE OF HEARTS

MOTHER

SETTING

Wonderland. This is not precisely the Wonderland of Lewis Carroll's stories, however. I imagine this as a more Victorian, more industrialized place. Think steampunk.

AUTHOR'S NOTE

Accents: This play is more fun if everyone has a British accent. The Caterpillar and Poppy can sound more modern, however.

ACT ONE

(A bucolic section of Wonderland.)

(Trees, bushes. Flowers. Strange outcroppings of rock. It's quite nice.)

(Upstage, three huge mechanical flowers, **POPPY**, **DANDELION**, *and* **PANSY**, *stand in a clump.)*

(Birds chirping.)

(The **DODO** *enters. Looks around.)*

DODO. Derp. Derp derp. Derp derp.

> *(The* **DODO** *approaches* **DANDELION**. *When it gets closer –)*

DANDELION. ROARRRR!

DODO. Aaaaah!

> *(The* **DODO** *runs off.)*

POPPY. Sweet.

> *(***POPPY** *high-fives* **DANDELION** *as best it can.)*
>
> *(A loud, weird sound shocks them.)*

PANSY. Aaah! Hide!

> *(The flowers cannot move. They hide as best they can.)*
>
> *(An odd, mechanical noise gets louder and louder, and then –)*
>
> *(Bang! Crash!)*
>
> *(A smoking telephone booth topples onto the stage [or is rolled on, or falls from the catwalks, or otherwise appears].)*

(*Smoke.*)

(**CARA**, *youngish, and wearing a leather jacket, stumbles out of the telephone booth, coughing.*)

(**THE DOCTOR**, *wearing goggles and a trench coat, stumbles out after her. He's covered in soot and dust.*)

THE DOCTOR. What was THAT?!

CARA. Sorry!

THE DOCTOR. Sorry? *SORRY?!* You hit a planet!

CARA. I didn't see it!

THE DOCTOR. They're large and round! This isn't difficult! I have never, in two thousand years, ever, EVER, hit a planet! I go around them. You see, I see one, there it is, it's a planet, shall I crash into it? No!

CARA. It came out of nowhere! I swear! I was minding my own business and boom there it was.

THE DOCTOR. Boom is right. Were you asleep?

CARA. No! Not entirely. I may have been daydreaming.

THE DOCTOR. You're not flying it again.

CARA. People make mistakes. It happens.

THE DOCTOR. You can be replaced.

CARA. You can be replaced too.

THE DOCTOR. The next girl – I want a smarter one.

CARA. Well I liked you better before!

THE DOCTOR. You're not alone! Everyone did. Even me. I liked me better before! But this is who I am now, and we're stuck! Thanks to you!

CARA. Where are we, anyway?

THE DOCTOR. Who knows? Undoubtedly a peaceful and happy land with nothing trying to kill us whatsoever.

CARA. Honestly?

THE DOCTOR. No! Death waits for us around every corner! Haven't you learned anything yet?! Look at this! A flower!

(He approaches the flowers.)

These are probably aliens. Or hallucinations. Perhaps they'll sneak up on us when we aren't looking. Maybe they'll summon Santa Claus, I have no idea. The only safe place is in the odd-looking spacecraft which we cannot name due to copyright issues.

CARA. Oh yes, the odd-looking spacecraft which resembles a telephone booth and yet is not a piece of intellectual property.

THE DOCTOR. Correct. We'll cower there until I can figure out how to get it running again. That's the only logical course of action. We hide. We lock the doors. We never come out. We talk to no one.

CARA. I'd like to look about, if you don't mind.

THE DOCTOR. I do mind! That is a terrible idea! I have no intention of coming to your rescue after you're captured by whatever beasts live here!

CARA. Stop being such a fraidy cat. The world is full of adventure! Let's explore.

THE DOCTOR. I'm not coming after you. I'm not rescuing you. I'm getting a new girl. Next reality I encounter – I'm going to find a pretty one, twenty-two, twenty-three years old, "Hey would you like to abandon your family and friends and go on an intergalactic adventure?" "Oi, that sounds lovely." "It is lovely, dear." "Are you single?" "Oh I'm afraid I'm too old for you." "Pity." "It is. Such a pity." She gazes into my eyes –

CARA. All right stop.

THE DOCTOR. Hold on. She gazes into my eyes – "I didn't realize it before now, but I've been waiting for you all my life." "That's what they all say."

CARA. It worked better when you were more handsome. The new face – trust me – no one's saying that to you.

THE DOCTOR. "Oh Doctor. What are you a doctor in?" "Let's find out."

CARA. I'm skeeved out now. I need to wash out my brain.

THE DOCTOR. Good! Maybe you'll discover how to be a pilot!

CARA. Oh go blow it out your ear.

THE DOCTOR. I plan on it, thank you. All right let's see if I can repair your damage.

CARA. Repair your own damage, first.

THE DOCTOR. You're very funny. You're hilarious. I'm going to go back inside and see what I can do. You. Stayyyy. Heeerree.

CARA. No.

THE DOCTOR. Yes!

CARA. NO!

THE DOCTOR. YESSSS!

> *(Pause.)*

CARA. Fine.

THE DOCTOR. Thank you. Stay.

CARA. Not a dog.

> *(**THE DOCTOR** goes back into the telephone booth.)*

> *(**CARA** looks about.)*

Stay! Oh that's nice. Stay.

> *(She talks at the ship.)*

You've become a cranky old man, you know! Stay. Here's a treat. Put it on your nose. It's not fun. It's not respectful. It's not like I haven't saved your life half a dozen times. I have. A few times this week, actually. And this place is perfectly safe. There's nothing odd about it at all.

> *(The **WHITE RABBIT** dashes in.)*

Well that's odd.

WHITE RABBIT. I'm late! I'm late!

CARA. Stay back! I'm armed!

> *(She searches herself for a weapon.)*

I may not appear to be armed, but I am! I know jiu-jitsu!

WHITE RABBIT. Oh dear! Oh dear dear dear dear dear! I'm late! Don't you understand?! *I AM NOT ON TIME!*

CARA. That's kind of funny when you think about it. How can you be "on time"? Are you on top of it? It's the fourth dimension, it's an impossible idea.

WHITE RABBIT. I can't talk! We have to go!

CARA. We?

WHITE RABBIT. She'll have our heads if we're late!

CARA. Well, actually, I was planning on –

WHITE RABBIT. No time! Come on!

> *(The* **WHITE RABBIT** *runs off.)*

CARA. That was curious.

> *(The* **WHITE RABBIT** *darts back in.)*

WHITE RABBIT. Are you not coming?!

CARA. I have a few things to do around here, sorry to say –

WHITE RABBIT. *(Strangely calm.)* Then I will surely die. And it will be your fault. I request only one thing. When I am gone, find my children, take care of them. There are several hundred. We've eaten a few of the smaller ones, but most have survived. I must go!

> *(The* **WHITE RABBIT** *runs off again.)*

CARA. Curiouser and curiouser.

> *(The* **WHITE RABBIT** *returns.)*

WHITE RABBIT. You're really not coming? You have no sympathy whatsoever? You'll just let me die? You heartless tart.

CARA. Fine!

WHITE RABBIT. Thank you!

> *(He runs off.)*
>
> *(***CARA** *follows.)*
>
> *(Crashing noises. More smoke from the ship. We hear* **THE DOCTOR** *as the lights change.)*

THE DOCTOR. *(Offstage.)* Come on now! This is intolerable! Who's your daddy! Who is your daddy! Ah!

>*(More crashes.)*

That's not even appropriate. I will fix you. I've had three wives say the same thing, you know. I will – OW MY FOOT!

>*(Crash crash crash.)*

I shouldn't have done that. I apologize. Now just one more little twist and –

>*(Lights up on a different part of the stage.)*

>*(A tea party is being set up. The* **DORMOUSE** *is lying asleep on a large table.)*

>*(The* **WHITE RABBIT** *streaks through –)*

WHITE RABBIT. I'm late I'm late I'm late I'm late I'm late I'm late I'm late I'm late!

>*(He's off the other side of the stage.)*

>*(The* **DORMOUSE** *yawns and stretches as* **CARA** *darts in.)*

CARA. Wait up! Stop your incessant running!

>*(She stops, hands on her knees.)*

I tried a 5K once. It wasn't pretty. I vomited. Not proud of that. Just a fact.

DORMOUSE. ...Hello.

CARA. Hello?

DORMOUSE. Are you here for tea?

CARA. I'm not, actually. I was following the rabbit.

>*(The* **MARCH HARE** *enters behind her. The* **MARCH HARE** *wears a suit with a bowtie.)*

MARCH HARE. Look no further! You are here for tea! Excellent!

CARA. Actually, it was a white rabbit I was following.

MARCH HARE. Not white enough for you, am I? Only have tea with white rabbits, do you? I see how it is.

CARA. No no no it's not like that at all. I'm British. We don't have these problems.

DORMOUSE. I find her offensive. In fact, if it were up to me –

(The DORMOUSE falls asleep.)

MARCH HARE. Not a problem. I'll have tea with you anyway. I'm generous like that.

(The DORMOUSE snores.)

CARA. Thank you. Is he...all right?

MARCH HARE. Not at all. But that's how we prefer him. If he were awake all the time, he'd be insufferable.

DORMOUSE. *(Waking up suddenly, mid-sentence.)* We'd chop off her head!

MARCH HARE. Dormouse, the subject has changed. We are no longer offended.

DORMOUSE. Oh. Apologies. There are times when I –

(He's asleep again.)

MARCH HARE. It's the narcolepsy. So sad. And yet so hilarious.

CARA. He probably needs medication.

MARCH HARE. We all do! It's much more fun to ignore that, though.

CARA. I can't stay for tea, though. So sorry. I'm following the white rabbit!

MARCH HARE. Nonsense! You are staying for tea.

CARA. Funny, because I just said the opposite.

DORMOUSE. *(Waking up suddenly, mid-sentence.)* – Have no idea what's going on.

MARCH HARE. Dormouse you've done it again!

DORMOUSE. What have I done?

MARCH HARE. You've slept through the important parts.

CARA. There are no important parts because I am leaving. Carry on with your lives.

(The MAD HATTER enters with a flourish.)

MAD HATTER. Everyone must be something!

CARA. I'm sorry?

MAD HATTER. So am I. Allow me to introduce myself.

> *(Pause.)*

I am doing it subliminally. Wait for it.

> *(The **MAD HATTER** stares at **CARA**.)*

It's no good you're an idiot.

CARA. I don't understand.

MAD HATTER. The very definition of an idiot. Who invited this mollusk to tea?

MARCH HARE. I haven't invited her, she invited herself! I tried to stop her.

DORMOUSE. It was a dismal failure.

CARA. Now see here. I have not invited myself to tea, I do not intend to take tea, I was following a rabbit and I will be going now –

MAD HATTER. We shall have to make the best of it, even though I hate her already. Sit sit sit.

CARA. No.

MAD HATTER. SIT!

CARA. Not a dog!

MARCH HARE. There's a dog? Where?

MAD HATTER. Too late! Tea has already begun! There is no escape. It would be rude.

DORMOUSE. Very rude. Awfully rude.

MARCH HARE. I might never get over it.

CARA. I am very sorry for all of you. I am rude, and I am leaving.

MAD HATTER. I like you very much already. You speak the TRUTH! Which I've heard is relative. But let me give you another piece of truth:

> *(Suddenly serious.)*

YOU WILL JOIN US.

> *(Pause.)*

Ha ha ha ha ha!

CARA. Ha ha ha ha that was terrifying!

MAD HATTER. I know!

CARA. I almost expected you to unzip your skin there and reveal your true nature!

MAD HATTER. Ha ha ha ha ha ha that would be mad!

CARA. Yes!

MAD HATTER. We're all mad here.

CARA. Right. Right. Well, good luck with that. And I appreciate the invitation, but I believe I was following a rabbit –

MARCH HARE. The white rabbit. She forgot to say white rabbit. It's a race thing.

MAD HATTER. We've got a rabbit here. He's not good enough?

DORMOUSE. I have an idea –

*(The **DORMOUSE** falls asleep.)*

MAD HATTER. Brilliant.

MARCH HARE. I find her offensive.

MAD HATTER. Then you must stay! I love offensive people most of all. I learned it from my mother. My poor, dear mother. She used to make armpit noises continuously. Every day of her life. She's dead now.

CARA. I'm sorry to hear that.

MAD HATTER. YOU DIDN'T EVEN KNOW HER! I'M OFFENDED! Wonderful. I love this. You must stay.

DORMOUSE. We chop her up into pieces and eat her.

*(They all look at the **DORMOUSE**.)*

That's not what I wanted to say.

MAD HATTER. Hold that thought. We'll make that Plan B.

CARA. Right. Again, this was lovely. And I wish you luck with your madness –

MAD HATTER. You must dress for tea! This outfit hurts me aesthetically. I am disturbed.

CARA. I think it's rather snappy actually –

MAD HATTER. March Hare. Put her in something better.

MARCH HARE. I shall!

(The **MARCH HARE** grabs **CARA**.)

CARA. Stay back! I can be very violent!

MAD HATTER. My dear. We can do this the easy way, or the hard way. The easy way – you change clothes, we have tea, we have a lovely time celebrating our un-birthdays. The hard way...

DORMOUSE. Plan B?

MAD HATTER. Plan B.

CARA. You don't seem so mad any longer.

MAD HATTER. Oh I am. But I'm focused. It's the best kind of madness.

(Short pause.)

Ha ha ha ha ha ha I love my job! I LOVE IT! GO! CHANGE YOUR CLOTHES! We don't want to have to eat you!

DORMOUSE. I'm an herbivore in any event.

MARCH HARE. Off you go.

CARA. All right then. I trust you have something in my size.

MAD HATTER. We can always make changes!

(**CARA** heads offstage.)

DORMOUSE. Might I propose a course of action?

MAD HATTER. No.

DORMOUSE. I do have a good idea.

MARCH HARE. You don't. You're going to fall asleep.

DORMOUSE. Not this time. I feel like I have it under control.

MARCH HARE. You don't. You're a liar. As soon as I say yes you're going to fall asleep.

DORMOUSE. I promise. I have a brilliant suggestion about the girl.

MARCH HARE. Very well what is it?

(The **DORMOUSE** is asleep.)

Dash it all! Dormouse wake up!

MAD HATTER. Oh let him sleep he's more interesting this way. Now, WE MUST PREPARE. Where is the tea?

MARCH HARE. Where it always is.

MAD HATTER. THAT DOES NOT HELP ME.

MARCH HARE. It's on the table.

MAD HATTER. Are you mocking me? Is that your plan? Mock me? Ha ha ha oh he's so funny. I'll tell you something, I have often dreamt of eating you.

MARCH HARE. And I you.

MAD HATTER. Really?

MARCH HARE. Oh yes.

MAD HATTER. What sauce do you think would be appropriate?

MARCH HARE. Vinegar.

MAD HATTER. Intriguing. I shall have to return to that.

MARCH HARE. Hatter, have you considered where this girl might be from?

MAD HATTER. I consider nothing and everything at once.

MARCH HARE. But, if she truly is...an outsider...the Queen might be interested.

DORMOUSE. We let some animals go nude from the top up. That way some animals wear pants but retain freedom of movement.

(*Pause.*)

MARCH HARE. You have ruined another evening.

(**CARA** *returns, dressed in a slightly gothic version of the iconic Alice dress.*)

CARA. I feel a bit odd.

MAD HATTER. You look odd. Freakish really.

CARA. I'm not sure this is me.

MARCH HARE. Don't worry. We're forcing you into our narrative!

MAD HATTER. It will be splendid! All you do is sit and drink and – what else is it we do?

DORMOUSE. I sometimes fall asleep.

MAD HATTER. We know!

MARCH HARE. We usually talk about politics.

MAD HATTER. It's a perfect conversation for the mad.

MARCH HARE. We pour tea and speak of the Queen!

MAD HATTER. You start.

(*They all turn to look at* **CARA**.)

CARA. What about the Queen? I'm sure she's lovely.

MARCH HARE. You're *sure* she's lovely? One hundred percent sure?

DORMOUSE. That doesn't sound completely sure to me. That sounds –

(*The* **DORMOUSE** *is asleep*.)

MAD HATTER. Oh he's dreaming. You can see his little feet twitch. I'm sure he's imagining he's in a field somewhere executing traitors. I'm sorry did I say that OUT LOUD?! I didn't meant to!

CARA. Traitors?

MAD HATTER. Oh yes. There are traitors everywhere.

MARCH HARE. Don't you agree?

CARA. Sure. Probably.

MARCH HARE. There are. People with very un-Wonderland feelings.

CARA. Actually, um… I didn't say this earlier, but I'm not from around here.

MARCH HARE. Go on.

CARA. I came from a ship. I crashed.

MARCH HARE. Crashed ashore, you say?

DORMOUSE. Eighty percent sure at best!

MAD HATTER. Where is this ship?

CARA. Um… I left the Doctor to fix it.

MAD HATTER. If you have a doctor fixing a ship it must be very sick indeed!

CARA. No my companion. Actually I'm his companion. The Doctor's.

MARCH HARE. Who is this doctor?

CARA. Actually, that's not his name. We didn't get the rights to Who, we're calling him What.

MARCH HARE. What?

CARA. Yes.

MARCH HARE. Who?

CARA. No, What.

MARCH HARE. What?

CARA. Yes. You've got it.

MARCH HARE. Got what?

CARA. His name.

MARCH HARE. What is his name?

CARA. Yes. You're right.

MARCH HARE. I'm asking what is his name!

CARA. I'm telling you What is his name!

MARCH HARE. Who are we talking about?

CARA. No! What!

MARCH HARE. What?

CARA. Yes!

MAD HATTER. Who?

CARA. No!

MAD HATTER. Who is the Doctor?!

CARA. No, What is the Doctor!

MARCH HARE. What is the Doctor then!

CARA. Yes! He's very confusing.

MAD HATTER. Who is?

CARA. What is.

MARCH HARE. What is what?

MAD HATTER. What is who?

CARA. In this version, yes. Doctor What.

DORMOUSE. Where is What?

CARA. I can't tell you where What is!

MARCH HARE. I still don't know who What is.

CARA. Try to keep up. We're not doing Who. We're doing What. Where is What? I can't tell you.

MAD HATTER. I've got it. I understand what she's saying!

MARCH HARE. What is she saying?

MAD HATTER. Yes! She's an idiot.

DORMOUSE. Does anyone mind if I sleep through this?

> *(Tries to sleep, can't.)*

Darn.

MAD HATTER. So you won't tell us where What is then? That's your defense? You don't know where What is.

CARA. I know where What is. I'm not going to tell you.

MARCH HARE. The Queen is always interested in new people in Wonderland.

MAD HATTER. She loves them! She ADORES refugees.

CARA. I'm not a refugee.

MARCH HARE. Do you have a job then?

CARA. Does anyone here have jobs?

DORMOUSE. I'm a crossing guard.

MAD HATTER. I'm a hatter.

CARA. Oh yes. Right. The Mad Hatter.

MAD HATTER. Do you know why I'm mad?

CARA. I haven't the foggiest.

MAD HATTER. I'm mad because people...lie to me. Girls lie to me.

CARA. Have you tried being more normal with them? Sometimes I'll lie to a bloke I'm seeing just because I'm a little creeped out. No offense, but you've got kind of a stalker energy.

MAD HATTER. I'm aware. It's in my eyes. You see them right?

CARA. I see them.

MAD HATTER. These are my lie detectors.

CARA. I'm not sure what you're getting at. I haven't been lying to you.

DORMOUSE. That's what a liar would say! I say we –

(The **DORMOUSE** *is asleep.)*

MARCH HARE. We've got a serious threat in Wonderland, you know. Foreigners.

CARA. Oh.

MAD HATTER. Sneaking in. Terrorizing us.

MARCH HARE. Drinking our tea without paying.

CARA. Was I supposed to pay?

MAD HATTER. Pretending they don't know that we charge money for tea.

CARA. I'm sure I have – I don't know that I have any money on me –

MARCH HARE. Right. No money.

MAD HATTER. And you're not even sure the Queen is lovely.

CARA. She is! I know she is!

MARCH HARE. Well, you're about to find out.

(They grab her.)

CARA. Help! Help!

MAD HATTER. Come along, Dearie! Time to see the Queen!

CARA. What will she do?

DORMOUSE. *(Waking up.)* Chop off her head!

MARCH HARE. Good one.

(They drag **CARA** *off.)*

(Lights change to the inside of the ship.)

*(***THE DOCTOR** *has a wrench and is trying to fix it, without much success.)*

THE DOCTOR. All right then. And...

(The ship makes a sad, definitely non-functional noise.)

THE DOCTOR. Darn. How about this? Yes? You like it this way, do you? If I touch you here.

(A worse noise.)

Tell me what you want then! You won't do it, will you? You won't communicate! That's what's wrong with this relationship! I am trying here, I am hoping to get you started, and you just lie there! Doing nothing! You think it's easy trying to get you started? I could have ten men with me and we couldn't get you started! Fine! I can find another ship that isn't a piece of intellectual property owned by the BBC! You think I can't? I'm an attractive man. Sometimes. I was before. Not so much anymore but next time I'm sure I will be. I'll be so gorgeous and I'll find a younger, newer ship. How about that? Huh? How does that make you feel? WORK! WORK FOR ME!

(He breaks down.)

I feel like you don't respect my feelings anymore. You don't care. You don't care that I've put my career on hold for you. For *you*. You haven't cared about me for years.

(He kicks it. An even worse noise. Perhaps smoke.)

Sorry. I didn't mean that. I'm so sorry. So sorry. I'm going to get some air then.

(He steps out.)

*(The three flowers, **PANSY**, **DANDELION**, and **POPPY**, are there, but otherwise the stage is empty.)*

Cara? Cara? Are you here? Come on, I need you to make the ship jealous. You're very young and pretty. I definitely need you. Not in that way. Sorry for the innuendo! I try to stop but it just makes more innuendo! Cara?

PANSY. HELLLOOOO THERE!

THE DOCTOR. Ah!

PANSY. Are you looking for that flower with two feet?

DANDELION. I SAW HER!

THE DOCTOR. Yes. Her name is Cara. You are flowers and you are talking. Seems about right.

DANDELION. Do you mind giving me a water?

PANSY. Don't do it. He's a dandelion. He'll put seeds everywhere.

DANDELION. Shut up, Pansy.

PANSY. That's the kind of talk I expect from a weed.

DANDELION. Take that back!

PANSY. Weed. He's a lower-class flower. Really. People chop him down.

DANDELION. I'll murder you! My children will rise up around you and choke the life out of your fancy little Pansy-pants.

THE DOCTOR. I'm sure this is all extremely important,

DANDELION. She called me a weed!

PANSY. The dandelion's just jealous because he's not cultivated. Oh! Did you catch that? That was a pun. He's not cultivated.

DANDELION. I don't want to be cultivated. Houseplant.

PANSY. I'm not a plant.

THE DOCTOR. Flowers. Please, I think you're both beautiful.

PANSY. You're going to judge me on my looks? Is that what you're doing? That's a stereotype.

THE DOCTOR. I'm sure you have wonderful medicinal qualities.

DANDELION. I'M LOADED WITH AMPHETAMINES!

PANSY. No you are not.

DANDELION. Eat dandelions and you'll be sky high!

PANSY. Oh stop. He has delusions of grandeur.

DANDELION. People eat me.

PANSY. They do not.

DANDELION. I'm on menus, Pansy! It's a thing now.

THE DOCTOR. Focus please! The other flower? The one on two legs? What happened to her?

DANDELION. I FORGOT.

PANSY. You'll have to ask Poppy.

THE DOCTOR. Who's Poppy?

DANDELION. That one.

> (**DANDELION** *points with one of his leaves to* **POPPY**, *who is staring off into space.*)

THE DOCTOR. Poppy? Hello Poppy? Are you in there?

POPPY. Duuuuuuuude.

THE DOCTOR. Hello. I'm The Doctor.

POPPY. Stay away. You don't get to use me.

THE DOCTOR. I don't want to use you. I want to learn something.

POPPY. Pull my bloom.

THE DOCTOR. I'm not doing it.

POPPY. Do it. Pull my bloom. Go on. Everybody's doing it.

PANSY. Oh Poppy. Please be respectful.

DANDELION. Don't try to change Poppy.

POPPY. Eat me.

DANDELION. Nobody eats you.

THE DOCTOR. Poppy. Did you see a girl named Cara?

POPPY. Ohhhh. I see a lot of stuff, man. Like, things that would blow your mind.

THE DOCTOR. I doubt it. I've been alive for two thousand years.

POPPY. Whoahhh.

THE DOCTOR. Yes. Exactly. Did you see Cara?

POPPY. Is she that flower with the feet?

THE DOCTOR. I suppose so, yes.

POPPY. Yeah I saw her.

THE DOCTOR. And?

POPPY. She was getting dragged off. Other flowers grabbed her.

THE DOCTOR. Other flowers with feet? They were taking her?

POPPY. I know, dude. That's what I'm saying.

THE DOCTOR. I'm just confirming what you said.

POPPY. I know. Crazy. We're on the same wavelength. We're communicating.

THE DOCTOR. Which direction did they go?

POPPY. It's like you're saying things and they're going into my brain. And they're like inside my brain now. Which is awesome.

THE DOCTOR. Which way did they go?

POPPY. Words.

PANSY. Oh he's getting philosophical again. We're going down the Rabbit Hole.

POPPY. So get this. What if we were all inside somebody else's head? Whoa. Like, there's a person having a dream? And that dream is us? Dude.

THE DOCTOR. In this dream, though, which direction were they going? That way or that way?

POPPY. Or no way?

THE DOCTOR. If she headed no way, she'd still be here.

POPPY. Wow. Duuuude.

PANSY. He's like this all the time. You can't reason with him.

DANDELION. You're such a Pansy.

PANSY. You're not a man, Dandelion!

DANDELION. I AM STRONG LIKE BULL!

PANSY. You're a little flower.

DANDELION. I AM A BIG MAN FLOWER!

THE DOCTOR. Please!

POPPY. If you want to know where she went, you gotta ask the Caterpillar. He knows so much.

PANSY. He does not.

POPPY. He's wise.

PANSY. Really isn't. That's an enormous lie. You just like him because he smokes you.

POPPY. He loves himself some poppy.

THE DOCTOR. Fine. Where is this caterpillar?

POPPY. That way.

THE DOCTOR. Thank you.

   *(**THE DOCTOR** heads off.)*

POPPY. Or that way.

DANDELION. I'm gonna cover this ground with seeds.

PANSY. You're disgusting.

   (Lights change.)

   *(A **WALRUS** enters, accompanied by the **DODO**.)*

   *(The **WALRUS** wears goggles, perhaps a helmet, perhaps a coat with many patches and trinkets.)*

   *(She is currently at work on a set of mechanical wings. The **DODO** stands nearby, chewing.)*

WALRUS. Scalpel.

DODO. Derp.

WALRUS. Scalpel please.

DODO. Derp.

WALRUS. Don't bother I'll get it.

   *(The **WALRUS** gets a scalpel.)*

 Wrench.

DODO. Derp.

WALRUS. Wrench please.

DODO. Da-derp.

WALRUS. Please hand me the wrench.

   (Pause.)

DODO. Derp.

WALRUS. Well if you're going to be that way about it.

   *(The **WALRUS** gets the wrench.)*

 And don't give me that attitude. I hired you, I can fire you.

(**THE DOCTOR** *enters, out of breath.*)

THE DOCTOR. Excuse me?

WALRUS. AAAAHHH! Stay back! I'm armed to the teeth!

THE DOCTOR. I mean no harm!

WALRUS. That was a joke. I'm a walrus. Teeth.

THE DOCTOR. Oh.

WALRUS. I should've said tusks actually. I'm armed to the tusks. Little walrus humor. I suppose it wasn't funny. I've failed again.

DODO. Derp.

WALRUS. Oh stop. No one appreciates you either.

THE DOCTOR. I was wondering if you could help me.

WALRUS. Get in line.

(**THE DOCTOR** *looks for a line.*)

There's no line. It's an expression. Still doing the humor thing. Still not working.

THE DOCTOR. Right. I'm looking for a girl.

WALRUS. Well, dearie...look no further.

(*The* **WALRUS** *spreads her arms.*)

THE DOCTOR. A human girl.

WALRUS. Oh. Right. Wouldn't want a walrus. We're not attractive, I guess. Doesn't matter that we can survive in frigid waters because of our layer of blubber. That doesn't appeal to you, I suppose. Not a quality you're looking for. Not into the blubber. That's all right. I can handle rejection. I'm a big girl.

(*She starts crying.*)

That's part of the problem, isn't it? I can't help it! I'm genetically designed this way!

THE DOCTOR. No no – I'm looking for a specific girl. A friend of mine. I have reason to believe she was abducted.

WALRUS. Nobody ever abducts me.

DODO. Derp.

WALRUS. That doesn't count. That was one time and it was no fun at all.

THE DOCTOR. She's about this tall and she has an angelic smile and so forth and so on.

WALRUS. Haven't seen her. She sounds awful.

THE DOCTOR. Or a caterpillar. I was told to look for a caterpillar.

WALRUS. Make up your mind.

THE DOCTOR. I was told the caterpillar knows things.

DODO. Derp.

WALRUS. Right.

DODO. Da-derp.

WALRUS. Oh definitely.

THE DOCTOR. What is he saying?

WALRUS. He said derp. Can't you hear it? Are you deaf?

THE DOCTOR. No I – Do you know this caterpillar?

WALRUS. And what if I did? Why should I tell you anything other than because you're so devilishly handsome? I've done it again, haven't I? Never mind. Maybe you serve the Queen.

THE DOCTOR. The Queen? Well uh... I'm not sure.

DODO. Derp.

THE DOCTOR. Are you friends of the Queen?

WALRUS. I should say not! She hires me from time to time to design flying devices for her. Dirigibles and so forth. But I hate every minute of it.

THE DOCTOR. Of course. Is that what the wings are for?

WALRUS. Oh these? Just a little side project. For my own amusement really. I'll fly about and then people will say, "Look, a flying walrus! That's something you don't see every day." And I'll say my name's Sheila. I don't really have a catchphrase yet. That's the best I've come up with.

DODO. Derp.

WALRUS. That's not it. That's a stupid catchphrase. Derp. This is why your people have gone extinct.

DODO. Derrrp.

WALRUS. You're right. That was hurtful. I apologize.

THE DOCTOR. Might I borrow those?

WALRUS. What for?

THE DOCTOR. I've got an idea.

> *(Lights change.)*
>
> *(Elsewhere onstage, the* **MARCH HARE** *and* **MAD HATTER** *drag in* **CARA.***)*

MARCH HARE. Must you drag your feet?

MAD HATTER. Hare, don't be insane. Of course she's dragging her feet. How are we supposed to drag her off if she's not dragging? That would be mad.

CARA. I'm not moving my feet anymore.

> *(She plants her feet.)*

MARCH HARE. We'll move them for you then.

> *(He reaches for one of her feet.)*

CARA. Hey! Get your filthy paws off me!

MARCH HARE. That sounded racist. That was racist, right?

MAD HATTER. I can't tell anymore. I just assume everything is. It makes my days so much more combative.

CARA. I feel like I haven't explained myself properly. Get your paws off me, quit dragging me, or I will crush you like bugs. How about that? Does that sound good?

MAD HATTER. I love similes.

CARA. Wonderful.

MAD HATTER. Here's one of mine. I will drink your blood like tea. HA HA HA HA! Is that good? Did you enjoy that? I am mad as toast. That one doesn't make sense. They're not all winners.

CARA. Can I go then?

MAD HATTER. Not at all.

(The **MARCH HARE** *reaches in to grab her, but she backs up.)*

CARA. Time to unleash the dragon!

(She makes a kung-fu stance.)

MAD HATTER. Dragon? It's found us!

MARCH HARE. Where is the dragon?!

CARA. Behind you!

(They turn – **CARA** *turns to run, right into the* **DORMOUSE,** *who grabs her.)*

DORMOUSE. I've got her!

CARA. Let go!

DORMOUSE. You'll never –

(The **DORMOUSE** *falls asleep with his arms around her.)*

*(***CARA** *tries to move, dragging the* **DORMOUSE** *with her.)*

(The **MAD HATTER** *and the* **MARCH HARE** *catch her.)*

MAD HATTER. Almost tricked us, did you? I love it. The Queen will love it too.

CARA. The Queen is a monster, right? She's zipped into a human skin or something? Or is a robot? Or a machine? Alien? Cyberwoman? Something to that effect?

MARCH HARE. You'll find out.

CARA. I hate it when people say that.

CHESHIRE CAT. *(Offstage.)* NOT SO FAST!

MARCH HARE. What was that?

(The **CHESHIRE CAT,** *equipped for battle, barrels in.)*

CHESHIRE CAT. ROOOAORORORR!

MAD HATTER. Ah!

CHESHIRE CAT. YOUR DOOM IS UPON YOU! YOU FACE THE CHESHIRE CAT!

(The **CHESHIRE CAT** *tenses to attack, wiggles his butt.)*

CARA. I'm saved! Over here!

MARCH HARE. *(To the* **CHESHIRE CAT.***)* Oh stop it. You're embarrassing yourself.

CHESHIRE CAT. NEVER!

(The **CHESHIRE CAT** *tenses again and charges at the* **DORMOUSE***. He bats the* **DORMOUSE** *in the head with his paw.)*

MARCH HARE. Stop that.

CHESHIRE CAT. No I won't.

(He bats the **DORMOUSE** *again.)*

MARCH HARE. Please. It's not nice.

CHESHIRE CAT. Can't help it, sorry.

(He bats the **DORMOUSE** *again.)*

It's in my nature.

(The **DORMOUSE** *wakes up.)*

DORMOUSE. Escape me now that –

(Sees the **CHESHIRE CAT.***)*

AAAAAAAH!

CHESHIRE CAT. ROOOARROARR!

DORMOUSE. AAAAAH!

MAD HATTER. AAAAAAH!

CHESHIRE CAT. FLEE! RUN FROM ME!

(The **DORMOUSE** *scurries away.)*

CARA. Yes!

CHESHIRE CAT. THE CHASE IS ON! I WILL PLAY WITH YOU BEFORE I KILL YOU!

(The **CHESHIRE CAT** *tenses, wiggles his butt again.)*

MARCH HARE. That is enough! Bad kitty!

(The **MARCH HARE** *baps the cat on the nose.)*

CHESHIRE CAT. I'm not afraid of you. You're a rabbit.

MARCH HARE. I'm a hare. There's a difference.

CHESHIRE CAT. I don't know what it is.

MAD HATTER. No one does.

MARCH HARE. There are important differences! I have longer ears and well-developed feet! Look! Look at these! Are these rabbit's feet?!

CARA. I think we've gone off the rails. You were rescuing me.

CHESHIRE CAT. Was I?

CARA. Yes!

CHESHIRE CAT. Ohhhh. I can see where you get that, but no. I was just trying to murder. That's what cats do.

CARA. So you're not like a Robin Hood figure then?

CHESHIRE CAT. More like a serial killer really.

MAD HATTER. Hare, let me handle this.

>   (*The* **MAD HATTER** *takes out a water pistol.*)

CHESHIRE CAT. What are you going to do with that?

>   (*The* **MAD HATTER** *spritzes the* **CHESHIRE CAT.**)

Aaah! Ack! Nooo!

MAD HATTER. Back!

>   (*The* **CHESHIRE CAT** *springs into the air to avoid the water.*)

Dance Kitty!

CHESHIRE CAT. Stop it!

>   (*The* **WHITE RABBIT** *runs in.*)

WHITE RABBIT. You're all late!

CHESHIRE CAT. It's a bunny!

MARCH HARE. Arrggh! He's a Rabbit! Rabbits and Bunnies and Hares are all different!

WHITE RABBIT. No time! No time! No time! We've got no time! I've got to get to the Queen!

MARCH HARE. Racist. We're all the same to you.

CARA. You're going to the Queen?

WHITE RABBIT. I have to go go go! Come on come on come on!

DORMOUSE. Aren't we going to do anything about the –

(The **DORMOUSE** *is asleep.)*

CHESHIRE CAT. I suppose that's my cue as well. I have to go. Ah ha ha ha ha ha!

(He tries to fade out.)

MAD HATTER. Are we waiting for something?

CHESHIRE CAT. I'm fading out, leaving only my smile.

MAD HATTER. I'd like to see that.

CHESHIRE CAT. Watch then.

WHITE RABBIT. Watch! Watch?!

(The **WHITE RABBIT** *takes out his pocket watch.)*

The watch says we're late!

CARA. Which watch?

WHITE RABBIT. This watch!

MAD HATTER. I can't watch that watch, I've got to watch this! It's not happening! Sometimes what doesn't happen is better than what does.

MARCH HARE. What am I watching?

CARA. He's not even here.

MARCH HARE. Who is?

CARA. What is.

MARCH HARE. Who?

CARA. No, What!

CHESHIRE CAT. Aaaah!

(The **CHESHIRE CAT** *disappears, leaving only his smile.)*

MAD HATTER. Well that's something you don't see every day. Unless you're mad. All right then!

(They take **CARA** *off.)*

(The **DORMOUSE** *sleeps.)*

(The smile is still there.)

*(The **CHESHIRE CAT** reappears.)*

CHESHIRE CAT. Forgot someone, did they?

*(He looks at the **DORMOUSE**. Tenses up. Wiggles his butt.)*

DORMOUSE. *(Waking up.)* The fact that the Queen kills everyone?

CHESHIRE CAT. ROAOAORROROR!

DORMOUSE. Aaaaaah!

*(The **CHESHIRE CAT** chases the **DORMOUSE** off.)*

(He returns with a tail in his mouth.)

CHESHIRE CAT. Guess he shouldn't have fallen asleep.

(He disappears.)

(Lights change.)

(Lights up on a strange part of the forest.)

(Huge mushrooms.)

*(Atop one, of course, is the **CATERPILLAR**, smoking his hookah. Sitting near him on the ground is the **MOCK TURTLE**.)*

CATERPILLAR. All right all right all right. Check it.

(Pause. He blows smoke.)

Yeah. That's it. That's it right there.

MOCK TURTLE. Can we please get back to my problem? I realize I'm paying by the hour, but still –

CATERPILLAR. Whoah. Whoah.

(Short pause.)

Whoah. That's not how I roll. I don't like...insinuations. I'm about respect.

MOCK TURTLE. Of course. And I was hoping you might be able to assist me –

CATERPILLAR. Oh yeah. Oh yeah. I am all about helping you with your problems. You don't even know, man. I'm working on 'em. Inside my brain.

MOCK TURTLE. Wonderful. So if I might begin –

CATERPILLAR. There is no beginning, man. None. Mind blown. Expanded. Waaaa...

MOCK TURTLE. And I appreciate that, but still...

CATERPILLAR. You're making "I" statements now. Consider... there is no I. You just got woke. You getting woke right now. Eyes. You got two eyes. Not one eye. I got eyes painted on me. Why? Why not?

MOCK TURTLE. I'm here about my relationship with my wife –

CATERPILLAR. I know.

   (**THE DOCTOR** *calls from offstage.*)

THE DOCTOR. Hello there!

   (*He enters.*)

You must be the caterpillar.

CATERPILLAR. Maybe. Maybe I'm just a transitional state before I reach a higher level of being. Butterfly.

MOCK TURTLE. Excuse me. I have a reservation... I have this appointment –

CATERPILLAR. It's cool.

MOCK TURTLE. It's not cool. I'm paying for this session. So you'll need to wait your turn, sir.

THE DOCTOR. I'll just be a minute.

MOCK TURTLE. Excuse me. Um...it's never "just a minute" with him.

CATERPILLAR. All right all right all right. Friends. I'm here for everyone. I'm like a mountain stream. Flowing.

MOCK TURTLE. Yes, but I am paying you thirty seashells an hour for this session and he isn't.

THE DOCTOR. Maybe I can just state my question –

MOCK TURTLE. No you cannot! I am a very calm turtle but I have had enough!

CATERPILLAR. Can I have those seashells now? Love them shells.

MOCK TURTLE. You haven't helped me! I am having problems with my wife!

THE DOCTOR. Your first problem was getting married.

CATERPILLAR. Oh yeah! Boom.

MOCK TURTLE. Stop it! Stop it! Listen! She has a problem with me being a mock turtle, I think it's a question of respect actually –

CATERPILLAR. So what's your trouble, Stranger Man?

THE DOCTOR. I'm looking for a girl.

MOCK TURTLE. She doesn't really respect me – "You're not even a real turtle! You're a mock turtle!" I can't help it! That's who I am. I don't go around saying she's not a real hippopotamus.

CATERPILLAR. Oh yeah. Girls. I know girls.

THE DOCTOR. She's a rather specific girl.

MOCK TURTLE. I shouldn't have married a hippopotamus – everyone said it wasn't going to work. She'll crush you. Are you listening?

CATERPILLAR. I'm always listening little dude.

MOCK TURTLE. Were you listening to me?

THE DOCTOR. Can we please stay on subject? I'm looking for a girl.

MOCK TURTLE. That's not the subject! That is not the subject! My wife thinks I'm half a turtle! She laughs at me! On more than one occasion she's threatened to turn me into soup!

CATERPILLAR. I've seen many girls.

MOCK TURTLE. Arrrhghg!

(*The* **MOCK TURTLE** *kicks a rock.*)

CATERPILLAR. But listen to this: What if the girl...is inside you already? If you look there first, you might find her.

THE DOCTOR. I'm certain that's not right.

CATERPILLAR. Then she's probably headed to the Queen's palace, man.

THE DOCTOR. Yes. The Queen's palace. And where would that be?

CATERPILLAR. It might be inside yourself.

THE DOCTOR. But it's not.

CATERPILLAR. But it might be.

THE DOCTOR. But it isn't.

> *(Pause.)*

CATERPILLAR. But it might be.

THE DOCTOR. Where. Is. The Queen's palace?

CATERPILLAR. Where it's supposed to be. Where it was yesterday. Where it will be tomorrow. It's in the same spot. But if you think of it cosmically...the earth turns, man. So today it's under the sun but tonight it's going to be under the moon. Is it in the same place then? I don't know.

MOCK TURTLE. I can help you.

THE DOCTOR. You know where the Queen's palace is?

MOCK TURTLE. Of course. I may be half a turtle, but I'm not an idiot.

CATERPILLAR. What is knowledge?

THE DOCTOR. What's actually my name.

MOCK TURTLE. What?

THE DOCTOR. Yes.

MOCK TURTLE. What's your name?

THE DOCTOR. Doctor What.

MOCK TURTLE. You'll fit right in here. I will tell you the location of the Queen's palace but first you must answer my riddle:

THE DOCTOR. Very well. Riddle away.

MOCK TURTLE. I told my wife I wanted to spice up our marriage and she put paprika on me. Should I be concerned?

THE DOCTOR. Yes.

MOCK TURTLE. That's it?

THE DOCTOR. What do you want from me? She's planning on eating you. It's obvious. Get out now. There you go. Relationship solved.

MOCK TURTLE. You're right.

THE DOCTOR. I know.

MOCK TURTLE. I think I always knew she wanted me dead. It was the little things, really. "I'm going to put you in soup and eat you." She said that on our wedding day. I thought it was a joke. "Ha ha ha that's funny sweetie." Then she'd say, "One day I will taste your tender flesh." I thought it was just romantic. My parents were right. "Don't marry that hippo she's a beast." "She's not a beast she's the animal I love!" "She's disgusting!" "You're disgusting!" "She's got eight teeth!

THE DOCTOR. Do you mind telling me about the palace?

MOCK TURTLE. What am I going to tell our children? Daddy has to leave because Mommy is hungry. My whole life is a lie.

(*The* **MOCK TURTLE** *breaks down.*)

CATERPILLAR. All right all right all right check this: A dream is a wish your heart makes.

THE DOCTOR. That makes no sense at all.

CATERPILLAR. I know. Which is why I say it.

THE DOCTOR. Can anyone tell me where the Queen's palace is?

CATERPILLAR. Yes. Most anyone can.

THE DOCTOR. Will you?

CATERPILLAR. No such thing as free will. I can't make those kind of decisions.

MOCK TURTLE. We got married at the palace!

(*He sobs again.*)

THE DOCTOR. Which is where?!

CATERPILLAR. Over the ridge.

THE DOCTOR. Thank you.

(**THE DOCTOR** *storms off.*)

MOCK TURTLE. The problem is, I don't think anyone's going to love me again. For me, you know?

CATERPILLAR. Right you are.

MOCK TURTLE. What?

CATERPILLAR. He just left.

MOCK TURTLE. What did you say?

CATERPILLAR. I did say.

MOCK TURTLE. I have to go.

>*(He leaves.)*

CATERPILLAR. So tell me about your problem.

>*(Lights change.)*

>*(The grounds of the palace.)*

>**(PLAYING CARDS,** *including the* **FOUR OF HEARTS** *and the* **SEVEN OF HEARTS,** *are manicuring the grounds.)*

FOUR OF HEARTS. First of all, I put in for overtime, and they didn't give it to me.

SEVEN OF HEARTS. I hear that.

FOUR OF HEARTS. Gary gave it to Two –

SEVEN OF HEARTS. Aww –

FOUR OF HEARTS. I mean, Two? TWO? I can understand giving O.T. to Eight, but Two?

SEVEN OF HEARTS. I hate Two. I say this to you – Two is my friend, but I despise Two.

FOUR OF HEARTS. I know he's having problems at home. But the card is useless. What can he do? He comes out here to paint the roses red – he can't do it. He's a waste. Nobody wants him.

SEVEN OF HEARTS. I thought we were painting the roses white.

FOUR OF HEARTS. We painted them white last week. That was last week.

SEVEN OF HEARTS. Ohh. Oh dear.

FOUR OF HEARTS. What have you been doing?

>**(SEVEN** *looks down at her can of white paint.)*

SEVEN OF HEARTS. This always happens to me.

FOUR OF HEARTS. No no. Don't worry. It's fine. We just start over.

SEVEN OF HEARTS. She's gonna tear me in half.

FOUR OF HEARTS. No she won't. Look at me. She won't. You're lucky. No one is getting rid of you.

SEVEN OF HEARTS. I'm just under a lot of pressure –

(*The* **WHITE RABBIT** *runs in.*)

THE WHITE RABBIT. Is she here? Is she here? Am I too late?!

FOUR OF HEARTS. No you're fine –

RED QUEEN. (*Offstage.*) WHERE IS MY HERALD?!

FOUR OF HEARTS. Ooh.

(*The* **RED QUEEN** *enters, with entourage, including the* **KNAVE OF HEARTS** *and several* **PLAYING CARDS***.*)

WHITE RABBIT. Her Majesty, the Queen!

FOUR OF HEARTS. (*To* **SEVEN***.*) Just stand in front of the white ones, you'll be fine.

(**SEVEN** *tries to hide the can of white paint.*)

RED QUEEN. Thank you. My Royal Subjects! It is a lovely day...for croquet!

KNAVE OF HEARTS. We're out of mallets, actually.

RED QUEEN. Out of mallets?

KNAVE OF HEARTS. I've procured flamingos.

RED QUEEN. You expect me to play croquet with BIRDS?!

KNAVE OF HEARTS. I've paralyzed them. They're stiff as boards. They'll work marvelously.

(*He takes out a flamingo.*)

See? Whack. Whack. It only hurts them a little.

RED QUEEN. I want them to hurt a lot.

KNAVE OF HEARTS. Oh.

RED QUEEN. My Royal Subjects! As you know, these are difficult times in Wonderland! Our kingdom is a disaster. Our dear King remains asleep. I wish there were some way to give you better news. But we are doing everything in our power to wake him. I fear...he may never wake up.

FOUR OF HEARTS. Have you considered a kiss from his true love?

RED QUEEN. I can have you killed.

FOUR OF HEARTS. Good to know, thank you.

RED QUEEN. But we must soldier on! Wonderland will remain strong. Please clap now.

(*Everyone claps.*)

Thank you. Thank you. And I know that in the past Wonderland was a more wonderful place. Everyone could have work. There was dignity. Animals wore pants. And little vests. We had strong values. We believed in each other. But that was before we were infiltrated by those who would destroy Wonderland!

(*Two other* **CARDS** *[or if you're short on actors, the* **MAD HATTER** *and the* **MARCH HARE***] drag* **CARA** *in.*)

We let them come into our land. We feed them tarts and cupcakes. We offer them tea. And what do they DO?! They want to DESTROY Wonderland! They HATE our wonderfulness!

CARA. I don't really mind your wonderfulness, actually.

RED QUEEN. SILENCE!

CARA. I'm just trying to set the record straight.

RED QUEEN. And they are CHEEKY! And do you know what we do to CHEEKY foreigners in Wonderland? CHEEKY TERRORISTS?!

CARA. Not a terrorist. I want to make that clear. I'm actually the one being terrorized at the moment.

RED QUEEN. MORE CHEEKINESS!

(*She turns to the guards.*)

Would it trouble you to put your hands over her mouth, please?

NINE OF HEARTS. Both of us or just one of us?

RED QUEEN. Figure it out!

> *(The* **NINE OF HEARTS** *and the* **FIVE OF HEARTS**
> *play rock-paper-scissors.)*

And hurry it up!

CARA. If I might say a word of explanation. I'm just a traveler – my ship needs repairs, and I will happily be on my way if you just let me fix a few things –

FIVE OF HEARTS. Best two out of three?

CARA. But I love Wonderland, I really do. Everyone has been very nice –

RED QUEEN. WHY IS SHE STILL MAKING NOISE?!

> *(Both* **GUARDS** *put their hands over her mouth.)*

THANK YOU. CREATURES OF WONDERLAND: You must be very afraid. Be afraid! The danger is real! This girl is a threat to us all! And I am the only one capable of keeping you safe! Ask yourself one question: are you on the side of Wonderland, or on the side of the evil dangerous terrifying FOREIGNERS?!

> *(She points at* **CARA**.*)*
>
> *(***CARA** *waves, tries to smile.)*

Take her to the dungeon! Tomorrow, OFF WITH HER HEAD.

> *(Everyone cheers as they drag* **CARA** *off.)*

KNAVE OF HEARTS. Truly brilliant.

RED QUEEN. And now, to distract you from my cruel dictatorship, SPORTS!

> *(More cheering as she raises her flamingo.)*
>
> *(The Dungeon.)*
>
> *(The guards drag* **CARA** *into a cell with a sleeping* **RED KING**.*)*

CARA. You're making a terrible mistake!

FIVE OF HEARTS. Again, so sorry.

NINE OF HEARTS. Just doing our jobs.

FIVE OF HEARTS. I've got little ones to feed.

CARA. How do you feed cards?

NINE OF HEARTS. That was a micro-aggression.

CARA. What?

NINE OF HEARTS. How do you feed cards? In our mouths! Where do you think you feed cards?!

FIVE OF HEARTS. Relax, Nine.

NINE OF HEARTS. I'm not that different from you. I'm just a card.

FIVE OF HEARTS. Let's go. She's not worth it.

NINE OF HEARTS. We could've dated. If we met in college. I would've been very into you. But now I'm not.

FIVE OF HEARTS. Let's go.

(**FIVE** *takes* **NINE** *off.*)

(**CARA** *is left alone with the* **RED KING,** *who snores.*)

CARA. Hello there. Excuse me. Excuse me.

(*The* **RED KING** *snores.*)

Are you...are you the Red King? But why are you in the dungeon?

(**HUMPTY DUMPTY,** *carrying a ring of keys, enters.*)

HUMPTY DUMPTY. Good question.

CARA. Who are you?

HUMPTY DUMPTY. Some call me...Humpty. You can call me Mr. Dumpty.

CARA. You have to understand that I'm not a threat to Wonderland, Mr. Dumpty. That's really your name?

HUMPTY DUMPTY. My parents were awful.

CARA. I know that you're enjoying this dictatorship – but the Red Queen is mad. I didn't have anything to do with your problems! I don't even know what your problems are, although, from looking at you, I'd say you were kind of fragile.

HUMPTY DUMPTY. Don't talk about my fragility! It hurts me inside!

CARA. That's fine. That's fine. And I want you to live a happy life. But I'm not a criminal.

HUMPTY DUMPTY. Not my problem, lady. I'm just doing my job.

CARA. But you have to understand –

HUMPTY DUMPTY. I serve the Empire, you understand? They have my family. There were six of us in the nest. Three were made into an omelet as an example to the others.

CARA. Must've been a large omelet.

HUMPTY DUMPTY. YOU THINK THIS IS FUNNY?! You think this is a joke! You sick witch! I watched as my sisters and brother were cracked over a very large bowl! You know what came out of them?

CARA. Was it a sort of yolk?

HUMPTY DUMPTY. Yes it was a yolk! They whisked them. They were *whisked*. And ingredients were added. Green pepper. Onion. Sausage. A little bit of basil. I watched the whole time. My eyes were open, if I have actual eyes, I'm not quite sure. I will never be whole again, do you understand? There are parts of me – broken. And they can never be put back together.

(He breaks down.)

CARA. I'm very sorry.

HUMPTY DUMPTY. Don't touch me! I'm hideous now. And if I don't want to be over easy, I'll do my job and be quiet.

(The **RED QUEEN** *and the* **KNAVE OF HEARTS** *enter.)*

RED QUEEN. There she is. Our visitor.

CARA. I demand to see an attorney.

RED QUEEN. You're demanding things now? How precious.

CARA. I'm not a terrorist! I'm completely innocent.

RED QUEEN. Oh I know. I'm not an idiot. I don't really care.

KNAVE OF HEARTS. Good one.

RED QUEEN. Shut your mouth, Jim.

KNAVE OF HEARTS. Shutting it.

CARA. If you know I'm innocent, why am I here?

RED QUEEN. *(Mock surprise.)* Oh gee I wonder. There couldn't possibly be a reason for jailing an innocent person, now could there? I suppose we'll never know. Jim, give us a minute.

KNAVE OF HEARTS. Yes, Your Highness.

> *(He exits.)*

RED QUEEN. He's nice to look at but quite dumb. That's why I put him in tights. I drop things. I make him bend over. It's lovely.

CARA. Is this the King sleeping here?

RED QUEEN. Is it?

CARA. I'm asking.

RED QUEEN. Why would the King be locked up in a dungeon?

CARA. I don't know.

RED QUEEN. It's a marriage of convenience, of course. He's conveniently asleep, so I'm conveniently in charge. You're convenient too, of course. Fear is a lovely motivator to keep the animals in line.

CARA. I'm not terribly frightening, you know. Perhaps if you drew fangs on me or some such.

RED QUEEN. If you tell a story well enough, anyone can be scary. Even little girls. You're scary enough to execute, of course. We'll make quite the spectacle of it. Everyone loves a good beheading.

CARA. I know that's not true.

RED QUEEN. I suppose the person being beheaded doesn't enjoy it.

CARA. You know you're quite different in private.

RED QUEEN. Really?

CARA. In public you seem unhinged and in private...you're quite hinged.

RED QUEEN. I love secrets. Here's one for you: I appear mad in public because the public is mad. It makes them feel better to know that their Queen is just as vain, stupid, and capricious as they are. Perhaps I'm wrong though. Perhaps the mad Queen is the real one and the one you see before you is a mad dream. Whichever. As long as I stay Queen, it doesn't matter.

(*The* **KNAVE OF HEARTS** *returns.*)

KNAVE OF HEARTS. All done? Have we passed the Bechdel test?

RED QUEEN. I was just explaining to Alice here –

CARA. Cara. My name is Cara.

RED QUEEN. Your name is Alice. Humpty Dumpty is going to chop off your head. And we're going to have the most marvelous party.

CARA. It won't work. You think you're the only person who's attempted to kill me? Ha. Ha ha! I've fought aliens. Real honest-to-goodness aliens. With laser guns. Robots. Killer robots. Statues that move when you're not looking at them. They all tried to murder me, and I'm still here. I'm practically invulnerable! Just try it. Try and kill me right now. Can't do it, can you?

KNAVE OF HEARTS. Shall I?

RED QUEEN. No, I'm curious.

CARA. Well I'm curiouser! And when the Doctor gets here, your little kingdom is going to go up in the flames.

KNAVE OF HEARTS. She's mad. Doctors.

CARA. He's coming. I have powerful friends. You ever heard of the Time Lords? They will mess you up. They don't care about your little kingdom, they're fighting wars across dimensions! That's right! I just explained the whole thing to you but you're too ignorant to get it, aren't you? We can fly! We can teleport! We have lasers! You are toast!

RED QUEEN. Who is this Doctor?

CARA. I'm not even starting that now.

RED QUEEN. Who is he?

CARA. He's your worst nightmare, that's what he is.

RED QUEEN. I have exquisite nightmares, child. You're living in one. Jim?

KNAVE OF HEARTS. Yes, Your Majesty.

RED QUEEN. Let's prepare a welcome for this Doctor who –

CARA. What. Doctor What.

RED QUEEN. Who is coming.

CARA. What is coming. I'd appreciate if you got the name right.

KNAVE OF HEARTS. What did you have in mind, your majestic wonderfulness?

RED QUEEN. You know what I have in mind.

> *(A weird roar from offstage.)*
>
> *(The* **KING** *tosses and turns in his sleep.)*
>
> *(The lights turn strange. Surreal.)*

RED KING. Mmmgh. Mrrrgg.

CARA. What's going on?

KNAVE OF HEARTS. *(Panic.)* He's waking up!

> *(The* **RED QUEEN** *rushes over to the* **KING.***)*

RED QUEEN. Shhh... Shhh... Go back to sleep dear.

RED KING. Mmrmmghg...mrmghghg...

> *(The lights get even stranger.)*

KNAVE OF HEARTS. It's no use!

RED QUEEN. Don't just stand there! Give me a tart!

> *(The* **KNAVE OF HEARTS** *tosses a tart to the* **RED QUEEN,** *who smears it over the* **KING***'s face. He struggles, but falls back asleep.)*

That's it. That's it. Sleep.

> *(The lights go back to normal.)*

*(The **KING** snores again.)*

CARA. What are you doing to him?

KNAVE OF HEARTS. Is it time?

RED QUEEN. Of course it's time. Release it.

(More weird roars from offstage.)

CARA. Oh dear that doesn't sound good.

RED QUEEN. I hope your Doctor enjoys the Jabberwock. I know it's going to enjoy him.

(Rumbling and roars.)

(Lights fade.)

End of Act One

ACT TWO

(The Forest.)

*(**THE DOCTOR** enters, using a kind of geiger-counter device.)*

THE DOCTOR. Almost there...almost there... And...

(He looks up. Sees the ship.)

And I am back where I began. Really? Really, universe? This is where I am? Over that ridge he says. What ridge? Which ridge? What are you talking about? Are you high? Why am I taking directions from a drug-addled invertebrate?!

(He talks to the device.)

Siri. Where am I?

*(The **CHESHIRE CAT**'s mouth appears.)*

CHESHIRE CAT. You're where you always were. Lost.

THE DOCTOR. Is there more to you or are you just a mouth?

CHESHIRE CAT. I am much more than a mouth. And much less. But actually I'm a cat.

*(The **CHESHIRE CAT** appears.)*

I can't help but noticing that you are larger than me. Therefore, I will not try to kill you. Not even a little bit.

THE DOCTOR. I have been wandering around and around and I can't seem to find the Queen's palace. Can you help me?

CHESHIRE CAT. I am a cat. So nope. We help no one.

*(The **CHESHIRE CAT** inspects his claws.)*

THE DOCTOR. There's a treat in it for you.

CHESHIRE CAT. I don't care in the slightest. Again. Cat. You're giving me a treat? Great. I will learn nothing from it. Do you mind scratching me above my tail?

THE DOCTOR. That's disgusting and I won't do it.

CHESHIRE CAT. That's disgusting and you will do it.

THE DOCTOR. I'll scratch you if you help me.

CHESHIRE CAT. Scratch first. Then I help.

THE DOCTOR. Very well.

> (*The* **CHESHIRE CAT** *approaches* **THE DOCTOR,** *sniffing his hand.*)

> (**THE DOCTOR** *scratches the cat about her tail.*)

CHESHIRE CAT. Oh yes. That's the stuff. Right there. Ohhhhhhh...

THE DOCTOR. All right. Enough. Where's the Queen's palace?

CHESHIRE CAT. I don't care.

> (*The* **SEVEN OF HEARTS** *enters, carrying a spear.*)

SEVEN OF HEARTS. I'll take you there. As a prisoner.

> (*The other* **CARDS** *[***FOUR, FIVE, NINE***] emerge, surrounding* **THE DOCTOR.**)

FOUR OF HEARTS. Don't make any sudden plays.

FIVE OF HEARTS. I believe this is what's called...a trick.

NINE OF HEARTS. I also have something to say.

> (*Pause.*)

THE DOCTOR. What?

NINE OF HEARTS. I don't know. There's a lot of pressure to come up with clever sayings. And I just... I froze.

FIVE OF HEARTS. We should've brought Ten. He always knows what to say. He's better than you, you know.

NINE OF HEARTS. Shut up.

FIVE OF HEARTS. He's always going to be better than you.

SEVEN OF HEARTS. Five. You're not being helpful.

FOUR OF HEARTS. Doctor What! You are under arrest for illegally trespassing on Wonderland. You are hereby charged with being part of a terrorist conspiracy to weaken the moral fabric of this land, steal tarts, and otherwise become a nuisance! You will be taken to the dungeons forthwith and so forth, until such time as you stand trial for your evil, wicked deeds!

SEVEN OF HEARTS. That was very good.

FOUR OF HEARTS. Thank you.

CHESHIRE CAT. Well... I suppose that's my cue.

> *(The* **CHESHIRE CAT** *disappears, leaving only his smile.)*

THE DOCTOR. There's only one problem. You seem to be playing cards and I am the greatest adventurer in the history of the –

> *(***NINE** *pokes him with a spear.)*

Ow! That really hurt!

NINE OF HEARTS. Sorry.

FIVE OF HEARTS. Why are you apologizing?! We're guards! We are terrifying!

NINE OF HEARTS. Oh.

> *(***NINE** *pokes him again.)*

Yar.

THE DOCTOR. Ah! Stop it!

NINE OF HEARTS. Never!

> *(Pokes him again.)*

I am the angel of death!

> *(Pokes him again.)*

FOUR OF HEARTS. Nine. Please. We are arresting him, not – annoying him.

NINE OF HEARTS. Sorry. Got carried away.

> *(Weird roar from offstage. The* **CARDS** *freeze.)*

SEVEN OF HEARTS. What was that?!

> *(Another roar.)*
>
> *(Two hearts fall off* **FOUR.***)*

FOUR OF HEARTS. Ah!

> (**FOUR** *covers himself.*)

> (*The* **JABBERWOCK** *enters.**)

JABBERWOCK. LUULULLULLUUUBLAHARGH!

ALL CARDS. AAAAAAAAH!

FIVE OF HEARTS. Beware the Jabberwock!

SEVEN OF HEARTS. I'm too young to die!

> (**SEVEN** *charges the* **JABBERWOCK** *with his spear.*)

> (*The* **JABBERWOCK** *savagely eats him.*)

> (*Perhaps a fake body is tossed around, or a giant playing card.*)

NINE OF HEARTS. Apparently he was wrong.

JABBERWOCK. LULULULULLLUUUULLRAAGHG!

NINE OF HEARTS. Anyone have a vorpal sword? Anyone? Is there a vorpal sword in the house?

> (*The* **JABBERWOCK** *attacks and eats* **NINE**.)

> (*His body is tossed about.*)

FOUR OF HEARTS. Mommy! Mommy! Aaaagghghgh! Mommy!

FIVE OF HEARTS. There's a Bandersnatch! I see a frumious Bandersnatch! And Jubjub birds! There's Jubjub birds everywhere!

JABBERWOCK. LLUELUELULULULULRRGHGHG!

> (*The* **JABBERWOCK** *destroys both* **FOUR** *and* **FIVE**. *Eats them.*)

THE DOCTOR. (*Trying to be calm.*) Nice...thingy.

> (*The* **JABBERWOCK** *looks at* **THE DOCTOR**.)

---

*Author's Note: The Jabberwock can really be anything. In my mind, I picture it as something like a Steampunk Chinese Lion controlled by two people with a moving mouth. You could also use someone in a Jabberwock costume or a giant puppet of some kind. Use your imagination. It should look cool, though.

I'm just a friendly Doctor wandering through the forest. No need to eat me or slobber me at all. Just a friendly Doctor going on his way.

JABBERWOCK. RARRHRHHGH? BLULLULULULU?

THE DOCTOR. Yes. That's right. No threat here at all. I'm your friend.

> (*The* **JABBERWOCK** *looks at him for a moment, then goes back to snacking on the bodies of the cards.*)

Sure. Do that.

JABBERWOCK. MMMRARMMWAM MWAM NOM NOM NOM –

> (**THE DOCTOR** *turns and runs away, and runs right into the* **MAD HATTER** *and the* **MARCH HARE**.)

MAD HATTER. Going somewhere?

> (*The* **MAD HATTER** *smacks* **THE DOCTOR** *on the head, knocking him unconscious.*)

We've got quite a party planned. Ha ha ha ha!

> (*He walks off, then returns.*)

Aren't you carrying him?

MARCH HARE. I thought you were carrying him.

MAD HATTER. I thought I made myself perfectly clear: You cannot trust anything I say! You're carrying him! You're the Hare! You have large feet!

MARCH HARE. That doesn't mean I'm a pack animal!

MAD HATTER. I'm not built for labor, look at me. These are nice clothes.

> (*The* **JABBERWOCK** *looks up.*)

JABBERWOCK. LLULLLULULELUELU?

> (*They both grab* **THE DOCTOR** *and drag him off.*)
>
> (*The* **JABBERWOCK** *goes back to eating the cards.*)

JABBERWOCK. NOM NOM NOM NOM –

> (*Lights change. We continue to hear the* **JABBERWOCK** *eating during the scene change.*)
>
> (*The Dungeon.*)
>
> (**CARA** *is chained up. The* **RED KING** *is still dreaming.*)
>
> (*Next to* **CARA** *is the* **GRYPHON**.)

GYRPHON. So I says to her, I have it on good authority that you've been eating the tarts yourself. What do say to that, your majesty? And she looks at me like oi – you're a freak. And I say, I was born this way, I can't help it that I'm part lion and part eagle. I don't even know how my parents got together to be honest with you. But that's neither here nor there. So I says, I may be a freak, but the people want to know the answers to these questions. That was dumb. So she looks around, she goes – "Do you want to know the answers to this freak's questions?" And everyone yells, "Nooo!" And I'm like, getting a bad feeling, right? She says, "What should we do with this freak?" "OFF WITH HIS HEAD!" That's not nice. Not a nice thing to hear. She says I'm gonna chop off your stupid eagle head and sew a lion head back on you. So I says, "Oh yeah, I'd like to see you try!" So that's why I'm here.

CARA. All I asked was your name.

GRYPHON. It's been nice. Being alive. A lot of magical creatures don't get that chance on account of them being imaginary. You don't see any unicorns around. You know what I'm gonna miss? When I'm dead? Conversations. I'm a conversationalist. They'll probably preserve my skull. Then I'll be a conversation piece. That'll be interesting. 'Course I'll be dead, what do I care? You suppose your brain can think things when you're dead?

CARA. I doubt it.

GRYPHON. Then how would you know you're dead? If I never know I'm dead, I'm basically immortal, right?

That's a nice thought. Like puppies. Love them puppies. So soft and tender. Melt in your mouth.

CARA. Would you be quiet please I'm trying to ruminate.

GRYPHON. Oh sure yeah. Of course. I'll be quiet. I love ruminating. I do that sometimes. Sit in a field. Ruminate. Ruminate again.

(Short pause.)

Not a lot of time for ruminating, to be honest with you. So many distractions. Noises. Little creatures moving about. Puppies. Mmmm...puppies.

CARA. All right. Please.

(The **MAD HATTER** *and the* **MARCH HARE** *push in* **THE DOCTOR.***)*

MAD HATTER. Why hello there! It's Alice!

CARA. Cara.

MAD HATTER. Look who we found.

CARA. What you found.

MAD HATTER. What?

CARA. Yes.

GRYPHON. Who did you find?

CARA. You found What.

GRYPHON. I don't get it.

MAD HATTER. If we don't get a chance to meet again before you die, let me say that it was a pleasure knowing you and I hope to meet you again someday.

MARCH HARE. She'll be dead.

MAD HATTER. Oh. Then we shan't meet. But we've already met. So I suppose that's something.

MARCH HARE. Something is better than nothing.

MAD HATTER. Nothing is also a something. If nothing was nothing you couldn't even think it, could you?

MARCH HARE. I love the way you think. Or don't.

MAD HATTER. See you at the trial! We're rooting for you! Off with their heads! It'll be fantastic.

(The **MAD HATTER** *and the* **MARCH HARE** *exit.)*

GRYPHON. Did you happen to bring anything to eat? A finger, perhaps?

CARA. You let yourself be captured!

THE DOCTOR. I didn't let myself be captured! I got captured.

GRYPHON. I fancy a bit of leg meat, actually.

CARA. Ignore him. He's a psychopath.

THE DOCTOR. I was trying to save you actually. The whole thing was about you.

CARA. Well that's wonderful. I'm so glad you saved me. Oh wait look! I'm still chained up.

THE DOCTOR. If you hadn't run off, / this wouldn't be happening.

CARA. I didn't run off, I walked off.

THE DOCTOR. Walked off then. Fine. If you hadn't walked off, you wouldn't have been captured, and then I wouldn't have been captured.

GRYPHON. I'd still be captured.

CARA. Nobody's talking to you. Well, do you have a plan?

THE DOCTOR. I'm working on it.

CARA. Oh. Lovely. You're working on it. Well, I hope it works fast because our trial is set for five minutes from now!

THE DOCTOR. Let's see.

(He begins taking things out of his coat.)

CARA. Why is it I have to be chained up and they let you roam about?

THE DOCTOR. Life is unfair. You can start crying if that'll make you feel better.

(He spots the **RED KING.***)*

Who's this?

CARA. The King.

THE DOCTOR. He seems to be doing a fine job.

CARA. He's asleep.

THE DOCTOR. I gathered that. Have you tried to wake him?

CARA. I'm chained up.

THE DOCTOR. You're always making excuses for yourself. Don't do it. You're capable of a lot. All right then.

> (*He crouches down to the* **KING.**)

Your Majesty. Wakey-wakey. Come on. Up you go. Wake up.

GYRPHON. Try biting him.

CARA. That's your solution for everything.

GRYPHON. Bite him.

THE DOCTOR. I'm not biting him.

> (**THE DOCTOR** *gently slaps his face. The* **KING** *keeps snoring.*)
>
> (**THE DOCTOR** *picks up the* **KING,** *he's still snoring. Moves him about.*)
>
> (*He pretends to use the* **KING** *as a mannequin.*)

"I'm the King. Rarr Rarr Rarr. Listen to me because I'm the King."

CARA. That's a brilliant plan.

> (**THE DOCTOR** *sets the* **KING** *down again.*)

THE DOCTOR. Not a natural sleep.

CARA. I think he's drugged. They smeared a tart on him.

THE DOCTOR. That sounds pleasant.

CARA. The kind you eat.

THE DOCTOR. In some cases you do that as well.*

> [*This line may be cut.]

CARA. Stop being a dirty old man. They smeared it on his face and he went back to sleep.

THE DOCTOR. Who did?

CARA. The Queen and the Knave of Hearts.

THE DOCTOR. I see. Curiouser and curiouser.

CARA. What do you think it means?

THE DOCTOR. Hopefully we'll find out. If we're not dead.

(Lights change.)

*(The **WHITE RABBIT** enters with a trumpet.)*

WHITE RABBIT. I hate to bother you but it's time for your trial! Oh dear.

THE DOCTOR. It's all right.

WHITE RABBIT. I faint at the sight of blood. It's going to be a very difficult day for me after your heads are chopped off. Oh dear oh dear oh dear – I'm not sure how I'm going to handle it! Seeing your headless bodies flopping about. Arms spastic. Blood like a geyser –

(He mimes blood spurting out of a headless body.)

CARA. That's enough. We get it.

WHITE RABBIT. Will you make sure to die very cleanly?

THE DOCTOR. I'll try my best.

WHITE RABBIT. You've made me so happy!

(Lights change.)

(Trumpet noise through the scene change.)

(The Courtroom.)

*(The **QUEEN** sits behind a judge's bench.)*

*(**CARA** and **THE DOCTOR** sit behind one table.)*

*(Various Wonderland denizens, including the **MAD HATTER**, the **MARCH HARE**, and **THE KNAVE OF HEARTS**, sit in the gallery.)*

WHITE RABBIT. Hear ye! Hear ye! I said hear ye! Please hear ye! Everyone! All right! Are we all listening?! Wonderful! Welcome to yet another fair and just trial of villainous scum! We gather today to investigate the terrible crimes of these evildoers, and try them in a just and perfect fashion! I would ask you all to remember that these criminals are innocent until proven guilty, which they surely will be. And remember that every time a criminal goes free, they will come to your house in the middle of the night and kill all of you! Are we ready? I SAID ARE WE READY?!

RED QUEEN. Get on with it.

> (*The* **WHITE RABBIT** *unfurls a scroll.*)

WHITE RABBIT. Introducing! The High Executioner! He wears a mask so you won't know who he is! But he is terrific! Here he is! Or she!

> (**HUMPTY DUMPTY** *enters, wearing an executioner's hood and carrying a giant axe.*)

HUMPTY DUMPTY. Hello.

WHITE RABBIT. And in this corner! With a record of thirty-eight and zero, all by execution, the mission of deposition, the one-man nation of cross-examination, the electrocuting, executing, prosecuting TWEEDLEDEE!

> (**TWEEDLEDEE** *enters, all business, in a suit, and sits behind an opposite corner. Everyone cheers for him.*)

His opponent! With a record of zero and thirty-nine, the mensch of defense, the correction of objection, the delirium, imperium, susperium, TWEEDLEDUM!

> (**TWEEDLEDUM** *enters, dressed like a fool. He waves to the crowd, then trips.*)

And of course our judge, Her Majesty, the Queen of Farts!

> (*Shocked silence from everyone.*)

> (*Pause.*)

RED QUEEN. Did you say Queen of...Farts?

> (*The* **WHITE RABBIT** *looks at the scroll, shaking.*)

WHITE RABBIT. There seems to be some kind of typo here. Even though it's written in script, but it says – someone – someone wrote this and I –

RED QUEEN. OFF WITH HIS HEAD!

> (*Two* **CARDS** *grab the* **WHITE RABBIT** *and pull him to the side.*)

WHITE RABBIT. What?! But I?

HUMPTY DUMPTY. Nothing personal Barry.

WHITE RABBIT. But I – It was a –

> (**HUMPTY DUMPTY** *raises his axe and brings it down on the* **WHITE RABBIT***'s head.*)

RED QUEEN. First order of business. We are in need of a new Herald.

> (**THE DOCTOR** *raises his hand.*)

THE DOCTOR. If I may.

RED QUEEN. You will not be the Herald.

THE DOCTOR. Oh no I wouldn't dream of it. I rise to offer some helpful advice. I understand that you want to present yourself as a ruthless dictator, and that's lovely and I don't want to step on your toes there, but perhaps you can do that without killing your employees? You see – I've got a lot of experience with villains. And frankly, they're always thinking, "If I kill one of my followers for disappointing me, no one will ever disappoint me again." And that's just not realistic. There's only so much talent out there. You might want to consider an incentive system. So...let's say your executioner here does a good job – you might say, "Humpty, nice job with the head chopping, I value your contribution to the team." And wouldn't that make him feel nice?

HUMPTY DUMPTY. Yes.

THE DOCTOR. See? You're inspiring him to follow you, not scaring him. That's leadership.

RED QUEEN. I will paint the roses red with your blood.

THE DOCTOR. Fair enough.

> (*He sits.*)

CARA. What was the point of that?

THE DOCTOR. I've just always wanted to say that.

RED QUEEN. Tweedledee? Your first witness.

TWEEDLEDEE. Thank you Your Majesty. I call...THE MAD HATTER TO THE STAND!

(The **MAD HATTER** *leaps up.)*

MAD HATTER. That's me!

(He scampers up to the stand.)

RED QUEEN. Do you forswear swearing?

MAD HATTER. I swear it!

TWEEDLEDEE. Wonderful! Now – when did you become aware that Alice was a dangerous criminal bent on destroying our society?

MAD HATTER. Before she even arrived.

TWEEDLEDEE. Amazing!

MAD HATTER. Indeed! I was in my home on Tuesday when I felt afraid. Now, I said to myself, am I being irrational? And yes, I was being irrational!

TWEEDLEDEE. And whose fault was it that you were being irrational?

MAD HATTER. Alice's! If she didn't exist I wouldn't have any reason to be irrational! But she does exist and I am irrational and I blame her! If she didn't exist I wouldn't be on this very stand right now explaining my irrationality! She's the cause of all of this!

TWEEDLEDEE. Certainly. Tweedledum. Your witness.

TWEEDLEDUM. Thank you.

*(***TWEEDLEDUM*** gets up.)*

What were you drinking when Alice arrived?

CARA. My name's Cara by the way. If we could set that record straight.

TWEEDLEDEE. Objection!

RED QUEEN. Sustained. The defendant will not speak.

TWEEDLEDUM. What were you drinking?

MAD HATTER. Tea. It was Tea time.

TWEEDLEDUM. Tea time? Time for Tea. I ask you – HOW CAN SOMEONE DRINK A LETTER?!

MAD HATTER. It's a drink. T E A.

TWEEDLEDUM. You expect us to believe that? YOU EXPECT US TO SIT HERE AND BELIEVE THAT THERE IS

A DRINK THAT SOUNDS JUST LIKE A LETTER?! THAT'S INSANE! WE'RE ALL MAD NOW?! IS THAT IT?! *DO YOU THINK WE'RE STUPID?!* No further questions.

(**TWEEDLEDUM** *sits back down.*)

THE DOCTOR. I'm beginning to sense why you lose.

TWEEDLEDUM. I have a good feeling about this one.

THE DOCTOR. How often do you have a good feeling?

TWEEDLEDUM. All the time.

TWEEDLEDEE. I call the March Hare to the stand.

(*The* **MARCH HARE** *runs up.*)

RED QUEEN. Do you swear?!

MARCH HARE. Never!

TWEEDLEDEE. Good! In your professional opinion as a professor of sociology, how would you characterize Alice?

MARCH HARE. She's a racist.

THE DOCTOR. Objection! That's an opinion.

TWEEDLEDEE. Facts and opinions are the same.

RED QUEEN. It is a fact that in my opinion opinions can become facts.

TWEEDLEDEE. How does it make you feel that she's such a racist?

MARCH HARE. Afraid. Very afraid. I don't know what she's going to do.

TWEEDLEDEE. I don't think anyone does. She's unpredictable.

MARCH HARE. She killed Dormouse.

CARA. What?! I did not!

TWEEDLEDEE. Terrifying, isn't she?

CARA. How did I kill Dormouse?!

TWEEDLEDEE. How did you know Dormouse was dead? The only way you would have that knowledge is if you killed him!

CARA. The rabbit just said I killed him!

MARCH HARE. I'm a hare, dang it! I'm a hare!

> *(He breaks down.)*

She always does this.

RED QUEEN. Could you restrict your questions to the rabbit?

TWEEDLEDEE. Of course. How did she murder Dormouse?

MARCH HARE. Dormouse was alive one hundred percent of the time before Alice arrived. He has been alive zero percent of the time after Alice arrived. Therefore, mathematically, it's proven that she is the root cause of his death.

TWEEDLEDEE. You can't argue with mathematics. Thank you.

THE DOCTOR. That doesn't make any sense!

> *(***TWEEDLEDUM*** *gets up.)*

TWEEDLEDUM. March Hare, is it?

MARCH HARE. Yes.

TWEEDLEDUM. That's your name?

MARCH HARE. It is.

TWEEDLEDUM. AND ISN'T IT ALSO TRUE THAT MARCH IS A MONTH?! HOW CAN YOU BE AN ENTIRE MONTH?! THAT'S NOT EVEN POSSIBLE! *DO YOU THINK WE'RE STUPID?!* No further questions.

> *(***TWEEDLEDUM*** *returns to his table.)*

Nailed it.

TWEEDLEDUM. I call Doctor What to the stand.

RED QUEEN. Who?

THE DOCTOR. What! What! We've been over this! What! My name is What! No! Don't ask any more questions! My name is What!

TWEEDLEDUM. What are we talking about?

THE DOCTOR. Stop it. Stop talking. Stop thinking. I'll answer the questions.

TWEEDLEDEE. All right then. Doctor. Would you say that you share Wonderland values?

THE DOCTOR. I would, yes.

TWEEDLEDEE. You would?

THE DOCTOR. Sure.

TWEEDLEDEE. What are Wonderland values? Can you describe them for me?

THE DOCTOR. Uh...fanciness and funny hats?

TWEEDLEDEE. A lucky guess. And yet you're not from here, are you? Coming from a foreign land. Coming to spread your foreign ideas. You want to change Wonderland, don't you?

THE DOCTOR. No.

TWEEDLEDEE. Did you or did you not say earlier, "That doesn't make any sense"?

THE DOCTOR. Yes I believe I said that.

TWEEDLEDEE. So you admit it! You want to make sense! You want to come to Wonderland and start making sense! Well we don't want to make sense here! Maybe in your fancy Doctor school they make all kinds of sense! Maybe they use logic to UNDERSTAND things?! Well I understand things without logic! I know what I know and I don't need logic to know that everything I know is right!

MAD HATTER. Here here!

TWEEDLEDEE. I say, you take your logic and you go back to somewhere logical!

(Applause.)

*(**TWEEDLEDUM** gets up.)*

TWEEDLEDUM. What's your name?

THE DOCTOR. Yes. My name is Doctor What.

TWEEDLEDUM. Doctor What.

THE DOCTOR. Yes. That is my name.

TWEEDLEDUM. And how did you get to Wonderland?

THE DOCTOR. I flew here in a spaceship shaped like a telephone booth.

TWEEDLEDUM. Your name is Doctor What and you flew to Wonderland in a spaceship that looks like a telephone booth?

THE DOCTOR. Yes.

(**TWEEDLEDUM** *processes this.*)

TWEEDLEDUM. I see.

(*Pause.*)

DO YOU THINK WE'RE STUPID?!

THE DOCTOR. It's looking that way, yes.

TWEEDLEDUM. That was a rhetorical question not intended to be answered! If you answer a question that is not intended to be answered it's as bad as questioning an answer that was not intended to be questioned! And THAT is unacceptable! No further questions, and no further answers.

THE DOCTOR. Question.

TWEEDLEDUM. No!

THE DOCTOR. Can I ask a question?

TWEEDLEDUM. You've already done it!

RED QUEEN. Get off the stand or I'll chop off your head immediately!

THE DOCTOR. Very well.

(*He gets down.*)

TWEEDLEDEE. And finally I call Alice herself to the stand.

CARA. I'm not Alice.

TWEEDLEDEE. I don't care.

CARA. I do.

TWEEDLEDEE. The clothes make the man. Those clothes make Alice. Therefore, you are Alice.

CARA. But I'm not a man, so the saying doesn't apply. You'll need to put a man in the dress.

TWEEDLEDEE. Very well I shall. It's not like I haven't done it before.

TWEEDLEDUM. Don't look at me!

RED QUEEN. Oh let's be done with this I have a croquet game to get to! Tweedledee, make your final argument!

TWEEDLEDEE. Oh I will! No you won't! Yes I will! You couldn't make an argument if it bit you in the behind! I'll bite you in the behind! I'd like to see you try!

> (**TWEEDLEDEE** *tries to bite himself in the behind.*)

In conclusion – foreigners are dangerous. She's a foreigner. Kill her.

RED QUEEN. Tweedledum.

TWEEDLEDUM. What?

RED QUEEN. What do you say?

TWEEDLEDUM. I just said what.

RED QUEEN. What do you say in defense of What?

TWEEDLEDUM. Kill the girl.

RED QUEEN. Thank you.

THE DOCTOR. If I may. I rise today to speak of –

RED QUEEN. Shut it! Where is the executioner?!!

> (**HUMPTY DUMPTY** *steps forward.*)
>
> (*A weird flapping noise.*)

CARA. Look there!

RED QUEEN. No! Nobody look!

> (*But it's too late. Everyone is looking and pointing.*)

HUMPTY DUMPTY. Now that's something you don't see every day.

KNAVE OF HEARTS. What in the world?

MAD HATTER. I'm going mad! More than usual!

> (*The* **WALRUS** *enters, with wings.*)

WALRUS. Hi I'm Sheila.

TWO OF HEARTS. RUNNNN!

> (*Panic. Shrieking. Everyone runs every which way, often colliding with each other.*)

RED QUEEN. ORDER! ORDER IN THE COURT!

WALRUS. Hop on! We're flying out of here!

CARA. Will we all fit?

WALRUS. Only one way to find out!

(**CARA** *and* **THE DOCTOR** *grab hold of the* **WALRUS,** *and she flies off.*)

RED QUEEN. AFTER THEM!

HUMPTY DUMPTY. Yes my Queen!

(**HUMPTY DUMPTY** *collides with one of the cards and falls down, cracking open.*)

AAAAAAAHAHHHH! NOOOOOOO! Aaaaaahhhhh...

(*The* **KNAVE OF HEARTS** *runs to him.*)

KNAVE OF HEARTS. Humpty! Are you all right?

HUMPTY DUMPTY. Uhhhhh... I'm not going to make it.

KNAVE OF HEARTS. No. You'll be all right. We'll put you back together again. You'll be up and doing your...Humpty Dance in no time.

HUMPTY DUMPTY. No. It's too late for me. Avenge me...

(**HUMPTY DUMPTY** *dies.*)

KNAVE OF HEARTS. No! No! Whyyyy! Whyyy!

MARCH HARE. Anyone else hungry?

RED QUEEN. No! Get after them! Bring me back Alice! I want their heads! Destroy them! Destroy them!

(*Lights change.*)

(*The Caterpillar's part of the forest.*)

(*The* **CHESHIRE CAT** *sits near the* **CATERPILLAR.**)

CATERPILLAR. All right all right all right. I hear what you're saying.

CHESHIRE CAT. I brought him the mouse. He doesn't even care. He doesn't even eat it, you know?

CATERPILLAR. Yeah.

CHESHIRE CAT. Why did I go through all the bother of killing it if you're not going to eat it?

CATERPILLAR. Word.

CHESHIRE CAT. This is my love for you. Here it is: It's bloody. It's in pain. It's making those little squeaking sounds. What more do you want?

CATERPILLAR. I hear you.

CHESHIRE CAT. I'm a cat, what else can I give you? Hairball? He doesn't want my hairballs. He says they're unattractive.

CATERPILLAR. He did not.

CHESHIRE CAT. He did! Unattractive! This hairball is me! It's literally me! I licked it off my back! How can you not love it? So you know what I did? I cleaned him.

CATERPILLAR. Don't do that. You gotta respect yourself.

CHESHIRE CAT. I hope it hurt. I've got a raspy tongue.

*(The sounds of the flying **WALRUS** coming in.)*

WALRUS. *(Offstage.)* Look out below! Hi I'm Sheila!

*(The **WALRUS** crash-lands in the forest, still holding on to **CARA** and **THE DOCTOR**.)*

I can't believe that worked! No one really believed in me and I did it! We flew!

CARA. Thank you! Now we need to get back to the ship and get out of here!

THE DOCTOR. Slight problem.

CARA. What?

THE DOCTOR. I haven't fixed it yet.

CARA. You had one job!

THE DOCTOR. Oh sorry! I was too busy saving your life!

CARA. She saved my life!

WALRUS. Hello.

THE DOCTOR. She only saved it because I told her about it!

WALRUS. I probably would've done it anyway. I like saving people. Gives me a warm feeling.

THE DOCTOR. You're not helping!

WALRUS. I did help. I used the wings.

THE DOCTOR. Yes you did thank you very much.

CARA. How hard is it to fix the ship? You do it every week!

THE DOCTOR. Well this time –

WALRUS. Excuse me. I couldn't help but overhear you since you're standing right in front of me. I can fix anything.

THE DOCTOR. It's alien technology, it's in fact rickety alien technology –

WALRUS. It's because I'm a walrus, isn't it? You don't think we can be mechanical. That's a stereotype. People think we're dumb because most of us don't wear clothes. Although I will say: most walruses are stupid. Really quite dim.

THE DOCTOR. I'm afraid it's not really a –

WALRUS. Oh sure. Sure. Of course. Well I'll just sit over here then. With my mechanical wings that I made from scratch. And these ecto-vision goggles I constructed. By myself. With no training. I'm just sitting over here with all my vast knowledge and ability being under-utilized. That doesn't hurt me at all. Walruses can cry, you know. There's a reason they call it blubbering.

THE DOCTOR. All right you can help.

WALRUS. That's very generous of you.

(*Thunder. Explosions. The lights flicker.*)

CATERPILLAR. Dude.

CHESHIRE CAT. Wasn't me!

CARA. What was that?!

(*The* **WALRUS** *puts on her goggles.*)

WALRUS. Near as I can tell, it's the fabric of reality unraveling. This won't end well.

CARA. What?!

WALRUS. Want to take a look? I made these goggles to let you see through the dream.

THE DOCTOR. What dream?

WALRUS. Our dream.

CATERPILLAR. Check it, dude. All this...is a dream. When the dreamer wakes up...poof.

CARA. That's mad.

CATERPILLAR. Right.

> *(More rumbles.)*

That's Wonderland.

THE DOCTOR. A dreamer? The Red King! He's the dreamer, right?

CARA. So is the Queen keeping us alive by keeping him dreaming?

THE DOCTOR. Possible. Sheila, I need you to –

> *(The* **RED QUEEN,** *flanked by* **CARDS,** *enters.)*

RED QUEEN. Not so fast!

WALRUS. We weren't actually going fast. I haven't found a way to do that yet.

RED QUEEN. Off with their heads!

CATERPILLAR. Dude. My head has been off for a long time. Sometimes, when I'm not thinking about it, it just rolls off my back.

RED QUEEN. Destroy them! Destroy them! Exterminate them!

CARA. Exterminate?

> *(The* **TWO OF HEARTS** *and* **EIGHT OF HEARTS** *advance, spears drawn.)*

THE DOCTOR. Maybe you ought to have a look?

> *(***CARA** *puts on the goggles.)*
>
> *(Big light change. Everything looks different.)*
>
> *(In place of the* **QUEEN** *is an evil pyramid-like* **ROBOT.**)*
>
> *(No one else is onstage except* **THE DOCTOR.**)*

What is it?

ROBOT. Exterminate! Exterminate!

> *(The* **ROBOT** *advances toward them.)*

CARA. No one else is real!

CATERPILLAR. *(Offstage.)* Dude. What have I been telling you?

WALRUS. *(Offstage.)* Just because I'm a talking walrus doesn't mean I'm not real.

ROBOT. Exterminate!

CARA. We've got to get out of here! There's a – I can't say what it is because it's copyrighted!

THE DOCTOR. Oh for goodness sakes!

CARA. It's an evil pyramid-like robot that was clearly built without much of a budget! Nothing else is real!

THE DOCTOR. I could've told you that.

CARA. Run!

ROBOT. Exterminate!

> *(Laser sound. Possibly an explosion.)*

CATERPILLAR. *(Offstage.)* Dude. Light show.

> *(**THE DOCTOR** and **CARA** run off.)*
>
> *(Lights change.)*
>
> *(The Dungeon. It looks very different.)*
>
> *(Only the **RED KING** is onstage, still asleep.)*
>
> *(**CARA** and **THE DOCTOR** stumble in. **CARA** is still wearing the goggles.)*

CARA. Hold on!

THE DOCTOR. I don't see anything.

> *(**ROBOT 2** enters and approaches the sleeping **KING**.)*

CARA. Do you see anything?

THE DOCTOR. The Gryphon is still chained up.

GRYPHON. *(Offstage.)* Puppies. So sweet...

> *(**ROBOT 2** takes a plunger out of itself and attaches it to the **RED KING**.)*
>
> *(The lights flicker.)*

CARA. There's a plunger. I hate it when it has a plunger.

THE DOCTOR. What has a plunger?

CARA. The robot thing has a plunger.

THE DOCTOR. There's a robot thing here?

CARA. Shhh... It's plunging the Red King. I think it's sucking out his dreams.

ROBOT 2. Extraction ninety-four percent complete. Estimated time of completion – seven minutes. Nineteen seconds.

CARA. Can you hear that?

THE DOCTOR. No.

CARA. Stop talking.

THE DOCTOR. Don't talk to me if you don't want me to answer.

CARA. Shhh!

(**ROBOT 2** *turns toward* **CARA.**)

ROBOT 2. Resistance detected. Calculating directive. Calculating.

CARA. You've got to wake him up.

THE DOCTOR. How?

CARA. Do I know? Find a way!

ROBOT 2. Resistance inconsequential.

THE DOCTOR. Where's the robot?

CARA. It's right there. But don't worry. It can't see you. We're inside the King's head, after all. It's not.

THE DOCTOR. It's on the outside of the King's head sucking out our souls.

CARA. Something like that. What do you suppose happens when it finishes the extraction?

THE DOCTOR. Most likely we die. Or, an alternate theory would suggest that our mental energies would be forever sucked into the robot collective. So we could live on as disembodied ghosts inside killing machines.

CARA. I always thought I'd go that way.

THE DOCTOR. Not if I can help it. Which I might not be able to.

(**THE DOCTOR** *approaches the sleeping* **KING.** *He's right next to the* **ROBOT.**)

So you're saying there's a robotic killing machine right here?

CARA. Actually to your left.

ROBOT 2. Resuming extraction.

THE DOCTOR. All right then. Lovely.

(*He gets over the dreaming* **KING.**)

WAKE UP!

GRYPHON. (*Offstage.*) Do you happen to have anything to eat? A leg perhaps? One of your arms? You don't need both.

THE DOCTOR. WAKEY WAKEY EGGS AND BAKEY!

GRYPHON. (*Offstage.*) Eggs? Have you seen Humpty Dumpty?

ROBOT 2. Extraction ninety-five percent complete.

CARA. Ninety-five!

THE DOCTOR. What's ninety-five?

CARA. They're ninety-five percent done.

THE DOCTOR. I don't need the pressure!

CARA. I thought you should know!

(**ROBOT** *and* **ROBOT 3** *enter.*)

ROBOT. Inferior lifeforms detected. Exterminate!

ROBOT 3. Exterminate!

THE DOCTOR. Ah! They're here!

CARA. You can see them now?!

THE DOCTOR. Yes!

CARA. Well this complicates my theory then! Are they dreams or are they real?!

ROBOT 2. Extraction ninety-six percent complete.

(*Something explodes.*)

(*The lights flicker.*)

(*Laser sounds.*)

THE DOCTOR. Come on come on come on WAKE UP! We need something stronger!

ROBOT. Off with their heads!

ROBOT 3. Exterminate!

(*The* **JABBERWOCK** *charges in.*)

JABBERWOCK. LULLLLULLULULULULU!

(*The* **JABBERWOCK** *attacks the* **ROBOTS.**)

ROBOT. Ah!

ROBOT 3. Retreat!

JABBERWOCK. LULLULULULULU! BWARRARRRARR!

(*The* **JABBERWOCK** *tips over the* **ROBOTS,** *or otherwise destroys them.*)

ROBOT 2. Extraction ninety-seven percent complete.

CARA. We have to wake him up!

THE DOCTOR. I'm trying!

JABBERWOCK. LLULULULULULU!

(*The* **JABBERWOCK** *continues thrashing the other* **ROBOTS.**)

(*The three* **FLOWERS** *walk in.*)

POPPY. Yo. It's time for my weekly appointment.

THE DOCTOR. Poppy!

CARA. What are you looking at?

THE DOCTOR. Flowers. We've got talking flowers! You can walk?

POPPY. When we feel like it. Pull my bloom. Do it. Pull my bloom.

THE DOCTOR. The tarts! The tarts came from Poppy! They're laced with drugs!

ROBOT. Extraction ninety-eight percent complete.

CARA. So?

THE DOCTOR. So!

POPPY. So...

PANSY. I keep telling him he's a bad habit.

JABBERWOCK. LLULULULULUL!

> (*The* **JABBERWOCK** *turns on* **PANSY.** *Devours him.*)

PANSY. Ahhhh! Noooooo!

THE DOCTOR. Stop that! Poppy! Poppy. Focus!

POPPY. Dude...

THE DOCTOR. How do you counteract your drugs?

POPPY. Wha...?

ROBOT 2. Extraction ninety-nine percent complete.

> (*The* **JABBERWOCK** *turns to look at* **THE DOCTOR.**)
>
> (*The lights flicker again.*)
>
> (*Booming noises from offstage.*)

JABBERWOCK. LLULULLU?

THE DOCTOR. No time! Who is the opposite of you!

CARA. The Dandelion!

> (**THE DOCTOR** *grabs the* **DANDELION** *and shakes him over the* **RED KING.**)

DANDELION. RARRRARRARARAR!

RED KING. AAAAAAAAAAAH!

> (*Lights down.*)
>
> (*Lights up on another part of the stage.*)
>
> (*The* **RED KING** *is standing in a pool of light. We are in his subconscious.*)
>
> (**CARA** *and* **THE DOCTOR** *are standing next to him.*)

Where am I?

THE DOCTOR. No idea, actually.

CARA. We were in Wonderland.

THE DOCTOR. Which was actually inside your head.

CARA. Metaphorically.

THE DOCTOR. Metaphorically inside your head.

RED KING. What's going on?

THE DOCTOR. What's going on is different than what went on.

CARA. Oh stop it.

THE DOCTOR. As near as I can tell, the robot things were feeding off your dreams in some fashion. Siphoning off the energy and using it to fuel their weaponry. Wonderland was simply a manifestation of your dream.

(*The* **WALRUS** *enters.*)

WALRUS. Hi there. Just wanted to let you know I've fixed the spaceship that in no way resembles a piece of intellectual property owned by the BBC.

CARA. Brilliant!

RED KING. Who are you?

WALRUS. My name's Sheila. I'm a walrus. A heroic walrus actually.

RED KING. Sheila? You were my babysitter. When I was little. You left me in a department store for four hours.

WALRUS. Ohhhh. I'm a trauma!

(*The* **MARCH HARE** *enters.*)

RED KING. And you were a stuffed animal I lost!

(*The* **GRYPHON** *enters.*)

And you're a combination of two pets of mine that were run over by a car!

GRYPHON. I am?

(*The* **CATERPILLAR** *enters.*)

RED KING. And you're my fear of drugs!

(*The* **MAD HATTER** *enters.*)

Then what are you?

MAD HATTER. I'm your fear of latent schizophrenia!

RED KING. I do hear voices sometimes.

MAD HATTER. That's me! We'll get more acquainted as you get older!

THE DOCTOR. I think our work here is done.

CARA. Absolutely.

RED KING. Then what are you?

THE DOCTOR. I'm not part of the dream.

CARA. We're real.

RED KING. How did you get in my head then?

THE DOCTOR. Probably a...

CARA. Vortex. Usually there's a vortex. We were sucked in most likely.

THE DOCTOR. Probably a result of the dream-siphoning machine. But I assure you, we are completely real.

CARA. One hundred percent. And we fly around in a telephone booth –

THE DOCTOR. And I'm an immortal timelord –

CARA. And I'm from the future.

(Pause.)

THE DOCTOR. That sounds realistic, right?

CARA. Sure. Of course. Completely.

THE DOCTOR. We'll be going then.

(They don't move.)

CARA. We're real, right? We're real people? We're not made up?

*(We hear a **MOTHER**'s voice offstage.)*

MOTHER. *(Offstage.)* Charlie! Charlie wake up!

*(Lights fade on the characters, including **THE DOCTOR** and **CARA**.)*

THE DOCTOR. Uh-oh.

*(The **RED KING** steps forward as **MOTHER** enters.)*

MOTHER. There you are, sleepyhead. Did you have a good nap?

RED KING. *(Stretching.)* Yeah.

MOTHER. I wanted to let you know *Dr. Who* is on.

RED KING. Cool.

> *(He turns on the television. Lights down.)*
>
> *(Theme music.*)*

End of Play

---

*Licensees should create an original composition or use a song in the public domain.

www.ingramcontent.com/pod-product-compliance
Lightning Source LLC
Chambersburg PA
CBHW070355120726
47909CB00008B/2860